His eyes flickered, turned jet black. He wanted her.

He squared his shoulders, towering over her, furious at her assault. "I do my job fine. But I can't and won't change my opinion about yours."

Her heart ached for him. "You deserve to be happy again, to move on with your life."

"My life ended two years ago," he said in a tortured voice. "I only live to catch psychos like you protect. And I don't need or want you analyzing me."

Emotions dried her throat. "What *do* you need?" she finally asked.

He stared at her so long she thought he wouldn't answer. The intensity of his gaze sent a shiver of heat rippling through her.... The hum of sensuality radiated off him in waves. He was undoubtedly the biggest, most masculine man she'd ever met, and he had needs, fierce needs that were driving him.

RITA HERRON

IN THE FLESH

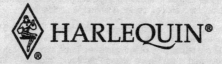

TORONTO • NEW YORK • LONDON
AMSTERDAM • PARIS • SYDNEY • HAMBURG
STOCKHOLM • ATHENS • TOKYO • MILAN • MADRID
PRAGUE • WARSAW • BUDAPEST • AUCKLAND

To my sister, who is the real therapist—
hope you find love again and your own hero.

ISBN-13: 978-0-373-69330-6
ISBN-10:   0-373-69330-3

IN THE FLESH

www.eHarlequin.com

Printed in U.S.A.

ABOUT THE AUTHOR

Award-winning author Rita Herron wrote her first book when she was twelve, but didn't think real people grew up to be writers. Now she writes so she doesn't have to get a *real* job. A former kindergarten teacher and workshop leader, she traded her storytelling for kids for romance, and writes romantic comedies and romantic suspense. She lives in Georgia with her own romance hero and three kids. She loves to hear from readers so please write her at P.O. Box 921225, Norcross, GA 30092-1225, or visit her Web site at www.ritaherron.com.

Books by Rita Herron

HARLEQUIN INTRIGUE

810—THE MAN FROM FALCON RIDGE
861—MYSTERIOUS CIRCUMSTANCES*
892—VOWS OF VENGEANCE*
918—RETURN TO FALCON RIDGE
939—LOOK-ALIKE*
957—FORCE OF THE FALCON
977—JUSTICE FOR A RANGER
1006—ANYTHING FOR HIS SON
1029—UP IN FLAMES*
1043—UNDER HIS SKIN*
1063—IN THE FLESH*

*Nighthawk Island

Don't miss any of our special offers. Write to us at the following address for information on our newest releases.

Harlequin Reader Service
U.S.: 3010 Walden Ave., P.O. Box 1325, Buffalo, NY 14269
Canadian: P.O. Box 609, Fort Erie, Ont. L2A 5X3

CAST OF CHARACTERS

Detective Raul Cortez—He's less than happy to be working with a psychiatrist. But when a serial killer targets her, he must protect her with his life.

Dr. Jennifer Madden—Will her vow to protect her patients' rights get her killed?

Marilyn Madden—Jenny's mother has been catatonic in a mental facility for years. But is she really crazy?

Bailey Madden—Jenny's brother fits the profile of the killer.

Dr. Rupert Zovall—The psychiatrist who has treated Jennifer's mother for years is upset that she's been moved to CIRP. Is he really worried about her or is he hiding something?

Clyde Anson—The court forced him to seek therapy through Jenny. But has he taken his sexually deviant behavior to a deeper level—murder?

Jamal Rakely—He murdered his wife but plead out on insanity charges. Is he killing women again?

Bobby Machete—A former patient of Jenny's—has he resurfaced from the dead?

Felix Brainard—He grew up in an orphanage in Savannah. Has he returned for revenge?

Eddie Keegan—Raul's partner at the force. This womanizer has always loved women. But when he gets rebuffed by one, does he turn into a killer?

Ralph Martin—The quiet, nondescript carpenter is renovating Jenny's house. Is his job a ruse to get close enough to watch her every move?

Prologue

South Beach, Florida

Some men shouldn't be allowed to have children.

He was one of them. Detective Raul Cortez, badass cop. Lousy husband. Son of a convicted felon.

Still, when his wife had phoned earlier to tell him she was pregnant, he'd nearly cried like a baby.

This was his chance at redemption. To make things right. To be a better man.

To have a future.

He climbed into his car and laid the red roses he'd just bought at the florist on the seat, heart pumping with adrenaline. Dark storm clouds obliterated the moon, indicating a storm on the rise, but he shrugged off the bad weather, started the car and headed toward his apartment. Nothing could ruin his day. Not a downpour or the fact that his latest collar, a psycho named Louie Mulstein, had been released on bail. He was under house arrest and had to wear that ankle bracelet, but the maniac should be behind bars. Damn shrink. It was her fault he'd been released.

Her words reverberated in his head. "He's schizophrenic, Your Honor. He's on medication now and not a threat to the community."

Raul had argued, had laid out the gruesome photos of the two women the man had bludgeoned to death for her and the court to see, but she had won in the end.

Tamping down his fury over the judge's and shrink's lapse in judgment, he vowed to forget work tonight. Anita deserved it and so did his unborn child.

As if to mock him, his cell phone rang. He checked the number—the precinct. The urge to ignore it teased him, but with two ongoing cases, there was no way.

"Cortez."

"Captain Black. Listen, Cortez. I hate to tell you this but Louie escaped."

"What?"

"Somehow he managed to get out of his ankle bracelet. We've issued an APB and my men are looking for him now."

Raul's heart thundered in his chest. Louie out of jail. Louie who was dangerous. A psychotic.

Louie who hated him. Who knew where he lived.

"I gotta get home," he muttered, then disconnected the call and sped up.

He swerved to pass a truck, turned on his siren and floored the gas, racing around the curve, his tires squealing as he spun into the complex. He honked at some teens on bikes to move, careened around the first building to the second, then threw the car into a parking spot and jumped out. Sweat trickled down his face as he ran up to his door. He started to reach in his pocket for his keys, but when he touched the knob, the door squeaked open.

Instincts honed by years on the force made him draw his gun. He held his breath as he tiptoed inside, silently telling himself he was wrong. Anita was safe. Louie hadn't had time to get to her. He wouldn't kill her, not the day he'd escaped.

But the metallic stench of blood assaulted him, and he spotted his wife's body lying on the kitchen floor face-up, her eyes wide-open in death, blood pooling around her head.

Grief and anger slammed into him, immobilizing him for a second. Anita dead…his baby gone…

A wail jarred him back to the truth. Louie was still here.

The scrawny bastard was huddled in the corner, knees hugged to his chest as he stared at the bloody knife. A sick sneer pulled his thin lips back over his teeth like a rabid dog as he lunged at Raul.

Raul didn't hesitate. He raised his pistol and pumped a round of bullets into the man, sending his body flying backward against the wall. Blood splattered everywhere, and Louie's choked cry echoed in the silence as he sank to the floor and went limp.

Raul collapsed beside his wife and screamed his rage. Blood soaked his shirt and hands as he pulled her in his arms and rocked her back and forth.

He'd killed the sicko. But it didn't matter. Anita was dead and so was his child.

And nothing could ever bring them back.

Chapter One

Two Years Later—Savannah, Georgia

Detective Raul Cortez stared at the pair of black silk panties tied around the woman's throat and cursed.

The Savannah Strangler had struck again. The third time in three weeks.

Another young girl dead. A blonde this time.

And they had no clues as to the killer's identity.

The sicko. He'd stripped her naked, strangled her with a pair of silk underwear, then left her posed in the woods in a sexual position with hands folded at her breasts and legs spread wide as if to make a statement.

Raul's partner Eddie Keegan lumbered up beside him, swatting at a fly buzzing around his face. "How long do you think she's been here?"

Raul shrugged and stepped aside as the medical examiner stomped through the woods toward them. "At least a day, but the M.E. will have to pinpoint time of death. Have you found anything on the other girls' computers?"

Keegan shook his head. "Not yet. I gave them to the tech guys to look at."

"We need to find out where he's buying the underwear."

Keegan kicked at a loose root. "The press is going to be all over us on this. Make us look bad."

Raul glared at him as he mentally assessed the crime scene for details. "Make us look bad? What about these poor women?"

"Hey, I *love* women," Keegan growled. "That's why I'm here in the damn woods at 5:00 a.m."

"Then do your job," Raul muttered. No wonder Keegan had had sexual harassment charges filed against him on his other job. "We have to find a connection between the vics."

"I told you the tech team is on it. But the guy probably just hooked up with them in a bar. Happens every night of the week. Something you'd know, Cortez, if you ever got out and had a social life."

"Some of us put work first," Raul snapped.

"Yeah, and some of us want a life, too."

A life to Keegan meant getting laid every night. He was competent enough, but Raul was tired of his sexist comments and disparaging attitude toward women. Keegan thought females had been put on earth for his pleasure, and that they all loved him. One day someone would put Keegan in his place. He hoped to hell he was around to see it.

Buckner, the new assistant M.E., shuffled up and knelt to examine the body. Raul muttered a silent prayer for the girl's soul to rest in peace, promising her in that same prayer that he would find her killer. Then he focused on the details—the way her body had been positioned, how the grass and brush looked around the scene, the type of tree that was nearby. Details that might not be important but ones that might prove helpful at some point, maybe in finding a pattern.

So far, all three girls had been left in wooded, deserted areas. No real significance except that it meant the victims hadn't been located immediately. Hiking vacationers or locals had discovered all three.

The killer hadn't sent photos or notes to anyone that they knew of. For his trophy, he took the girl's underwear.

The crime-scene unit was taking photographs, although Raul had snapped a few of his own when he'd arrived. He had been first on the scene, had secured the area and had searched for footprints but found nothing but some crushed dead plants and a few broken twigs. It had recently rained, which made finding evidence more difficult, but he still held out hope that the CSI team might find something. A piece of clothing, hair, a shoe print…anything they could trace.

Captain Black approached, wearing a grim expression. "Damn. It looks like we may have to call in the feds."

Words Raul didn't want to hear. "Give us another week."

Black shrugged. "I already talked to a friend of mine at the bureau. It'll take that long to get someone out here. I asked for a profiler, but he suggested a local counselor that he thought could help us. A sex therapist named Jenny Madden."

"Not a shrink," Raul mumbled.

Black arched a brow. "I know your history, Cortez, but we have to use every available resource. If it means bringing in a counselor or psychiatrist, then we'll do it."

Raul grimaced. Black could do what he wanted. But no way in hell was he ever going to trust a shrink again or take her word on anything.

He'd solve the damn case without her.

DR. JENNY MADDEN took a deep breath before entering her mother's hospital room at CIRP, the Coastal Island

Research Park mental facility. She reserved Sunday mornings to visit—not that her mother displayed signs of being aware of her presence—but Jenny's conscience and her heart wouldn't allow her to be anywhere else.

After all, Sundays had been about family when they were growing up: a big breakfast of pancakes or home-made cinnamon rolls; hurriedly dressing for church, putting on the Sunday dress her mother had made, her lacy Sunday socks and patent leather shoes; Bailey, her little brother, grumbling and complaining but her mother dragging him along anyway, saying his protests meant that he needed it.

Emotions crowded her chest. Her parents had been such a handsome couple. At least for the first six years of her life. Then one day everything had fallen apart.

Pain sucked the air from her lungs as she remembered hearing her mother's screams the night he'd walked out. The terrible fight, her mother chasing after him. Her father's car spewing dust as he drove away and never came back.

She brushed at a tear, wishing for once that she could think of that day or visit her mother without her heart breaking, but twenty years later the memory was fresh and raw like an open wound that wouldn't heal.

Forcing herself to regain control, she inhaled the scent of the daffodils she held in one hand along with the fresh cinnamon rolls from the bakery, hoping they would evoke fond memories for her mother and miraculously open the doors of communication. Although hope was fledgling these days. After all, years of silence would probably not be broken by cinnamon rolls or flowers.

Determined to present a cheery picture, she pasted on a smile, pushed open the door and waved as she entered the room. "Hi, Mom. I brought flowers and those cinnamon rolls you like so much."

Her mother lay propped against the bed pillows, her now-graying brown hair tangled, her mouth drooping slightly to the left as she stared into space.

"I'll just put these in fresh water," Jenny said. "Then we'll get you a bath and I'll brush your hair before we have breakfast."

Her mother said nothing, but Jenny tacked a smile on her face, put the flowers in water, then placed them on the small table across from her mother so she could see them.

"Which gown would you like to wear today?" She plucked a lavender one from the drawer, along with its matching bed jacket. "How about this one? Lavender looks so pretty on you, Mom. Remember that lavender dress you wore to church on Easter when I was ten?" She filled the basin with water, poured in scented bath gel and gave her mother a sponge bath. Her mother made a soft whispery sound as if she enjoyed the process. "What is it, Mom? You want to talk to me. I know you do."

Then the second passed, and that empty gray look returned to her eyes. Jenny willed the lump in her throat to dissipate, and turned away to gather her composure. She emptied the bathwater, then returned with the brush, sat down beside her mother and began to slowly work the tangles from her hair. Her mother sighed contentedly. Twice during this ritual she'd reached out and touched Jenny's hand and squeezed it.

At that moment she'd known her mother was still inside the shell of her body. That she wanted to talk but something was holding her back.

Jenny had become a doctor to find the answer.

Unfortunately, her education and experience had yet to yield results. The very reason she'd moved her mother to CIRP. Hopefully, the psychiatrists at the center would find a treatment for her that would prove successful.

Dr. Zovall hadn't been happy about the move. He'd been treating her mother for years, and had been a friend to her parents before the breakdown. A bigger friend since. He mourned her mother's loss almost as much as Jenny and her brother, Bailey, did.

Yet he hadn't been able to help her....

She counted the strokes as she glided the brush through her mother's hair, a hundred strokes just as her mother used to do for her when she was little, sweeping her hair down over her shoulders until it lay in soft folds. "There, you look lovely now, Mom."

She helped her mother settle back, inserted a jazz CD in the portable player, then set out their breakfast. Coffee for her, juice for her mother. Her mother nibbled at the food with no reaction, but ate the cinnamon roll and even licked her fingers when she finished. Jenny chatted about her week, telling her about the small house she'd bought in downtown Savannah, about the renovations, all mundane details, but if her mother could hear, she wanted to include her in her life.

Her cell phone vibrated against her belt, and she frowned and checked the number. The hospital. Darn it, there must be an emergency.

"Mom, I have to take this," Jenny said, then she kissed her cheek and stepped into the hallway.

"Dr. Madden, this is the emergency service. Captain Black with the Savannah Police Department needs to speak with you as soon as possible."

Jenny clenched the phone with sweaty fingers. Was one of her patients in trouble? Had one of them been hurt or committed a crime? "Did he say what it was about?"

"No, he just said he needed to talk to you, today if possible."

"I'll give him a call right now."

She hung up, then phoned the police precinct. Seconds later, they patched her through to his cell phone. "This is Dr. Madden. How can I help you, Captain Black?"

"We found a murdered girl this morning, same MO as the two other strangled victims."

"You think it's a serial killer?" Jenny asked.

"Yes. And you come highly recommended."

"I'll do whatever I can to help."

"Can you meet me at the crime scene?"

"Sure. Let me have the address." He gave it to her, and she ducked in and said goodbye to her mother. "I'll try to stop back this week, Mom. I love you." She squeezed her hands and hoped for a response, but her mother closed her eyes as if exhausted and drifted to sleep. Jenny left, her heart in her throat.

She had attended a few crime scenes for consultant work, but it was not her favorite part of the job. Shadows from the live oaks flickered along the road as she drove to the wooded area and parked along the side of the road by the police vehicles. She took one look at her clothes and wished she'd gone home to change. The loose skirt and sandals weren't exactly conducive to hiking. Yet she hadn't wanted to make the police wait, not when the captain seemed eager for her assistance, when he was obviously frustrated over losing another girl.

Had the captain called her because he wanted her help in putting together a profile, or did he have a suspect?

And why her specifically? Did he have reason to believe that one of her patients might be the killer?

RAUL SAW the baby-blue Beetle convertible swing in beside the squad car and grimaced from his post at the edge of the woods. Had to be Jenny Madden—*Dr.* Jenny Madden.

He'd half expected her to be driving a Porsche or Beamer, but the tiny convertible suited his image of her, as well. A girly-girl car.

She was probably rich, prissy, earned ten times his yearly salary and thought she knew it all.

He hoped to hell she didn't puke when she saw the body. Already the flies and bugs had feasted, and the stench had gotten bad. At least CSI was almost finished, so if she lost it, she wouldn't contaminate evidence.

Before she cut the engine, she dragged a brush through her hair. Concerned about her looks at a crime scene—not a good sign.

He tried not to notice the long silky-looking blond strands but couldn't help himself as she pulled them back into a ponytail at the base of her neck. Then she climbed out and his gut clenched at the sight of that body. High full breasts tapered to a slender waist. She wore a dark-blue tank top that clung to her figure in the cloying summer heat, and a loose white skirt that swirled around her slender ankles, leading his eyes down to her sandaled feet and toenails painted a hot red.

Damn. He liked red toenails.

He dragged his gaze back up to her face, searching for the flaw. Unfortunately, he didn't see one on the surface. Soft features shaped a dainty nose and high sculpted cheekbones, and her lips were pouty and pink, natural, no lipstick.

She would have to be a knockout. Long blond hair and longer legs that could grip a man and make him crazy. Yep, the devil always came disguised in pretty packages.

Not that he would let her model looks distract him from the job or make him forget what she was. A shrink.

An interference in the case.

He didn't know why Black had insisted on calling her out here. A short but sweet meeting at the precinct would have sufficed. And worse, the captain had ordered *him* to babysit her to the scene.

She started toward the woods, and he cleared his throat. "You can't go that way. This is a crime scene."

She startled and almost lost her footing, and he cursed the fact that she didn't have enough sense to dress appropriately for the woods.

"I didn't see you skulking in the shadows," she said, jutting up her chin.

He almost laughed. He'd expected a sweet voice to go with that body. Instead, it was husky, and her glare so sharp that it cut to the bone. "Are you *Dr.* Madden?"

She nodded. "Captain Black *requested* I come."

He gave a clipped nod, biting back the fact that he disagreed with his superior. The last thing he wanted was to get pulled from the investigation because of his personal dislike for her. "I'm supposed to escort you to the crime scene."

She wet her lip, a sign of nervousness, but he refused to cut her any slack. If she couldn't do the job, then Black should see it now, so they'd be done with this crap and he wouldn't have to deal with her.

"And you are?" she asked.

"Detective Raul Cortez." He gestured toward the path to his left. "Follow me. The body is this way."

He didn't wait on her response, but strode into the woods. He heard the brush parting, twigs snapping beneath her feet, her breathing labored as she hurried behind him, but he didn't slow down until he heard her yelp.

He inhaled sharply and pivoted, frowning as she gripped a tree trunk and massaged her foot.

A second of remorse filled him for being curt, but this job was not for sissies. "You should have dressed for work instead of the country club."

She fisted her hands by her side. "I was already out when I received the call."

"A champagne brunch, no doubt."

"Frankly that's none of your business." She flicked her hand forward. "Just lead the way. I'll keep up."

The challenge in her tone egged him on, and he stalked the rest of the way, not breaking stride until he reached the crime scene tape. The CSI team had scattered, searching the surrounding area, and Black was waiting beside the body. He wanted Dr. Madden to see the way she'd been posed to get the full effect of this perp's MO.

Black frowned at Raul as the doctor trotted behind him. He made no excuse, but turned and gestured in introduction. "Dr. Madden, Captain Black."

Black extended his hand. "Thank you for coming, Dr. Madden. My friend Agent Steele and his wife, Claire, recommended you."

The woman smiled. "Yes, I worked with Claire before. I can't believe she's married now and has two kids."

"We're not interested in chitchating about your friends' families," Raul cut in.

She whirled on him. "Yes, I can see that you wouldn't, you're probably not a family man."

A muscle ticked in his jaw. "As you can see, we have a dead woman on our hands," he snapped.

"Detective," Black said in a warning tone.

Jenny threw up a hand. "It's all right. I'm sorry to hear another girl has been murdered."

Black clenched his jaw. "Yeah. We have to find this guy before he strikes again."

She slanted her gaze toward the body, and her expression softened. "You're right. Let's get to work."

Raul grunted, and she gave him a glacier look but refrained from comment as she addressed Black. "Do you want to tell me the details first or want me to assess the situation for myself?"

"Why don't you look first, then give us your thoughts," Black said. "We want your gut reaction, your unbiased, professional opinion."

Raul frowned at the word *we* but knew better than to argue, so he kept his mouth shut. Instead he braced himself to steer the woman to the side if she got sick, or to catch her if she passed out.

Hell, he halfway hoped she did. Then Black could see she didn't belong here, and they'd be rid of her.

Chapter Two

Jenny tried to tamp down her anger at Detective Raul Cortez. Even though he was easy on the eyes, he was rude, insolent, and the perfect example of why some people called policemen pigs.

She was accustomed to some adversity, but no one had ever taken such an instant dislike to her before. If she didn't have a job to do here, her feelings might be hurt.

Or she might spit in his face and walk away.

But Jenny had never backed down from a fight or let anyone bully her, and plenty of male patients had tried. She sure as heck didn't intend to play scaredy-cat now.

Irritation at the detective morphed into horror and anger at the person who'd killed this girl as she picked her way through the weeds and spotted the body. The detective and Captain Black eased up beside her. Cortez was probably waiting for her to fall apart so he could laugh in her face.

She refused to give him the pleasure.

Forcing a calm to her expression that belied the trembling inside her, she knelt by the woman and mentally made notes of the scene. She was young, mid-twenties probably, blond, and she'd been strangled to death with a pair of silk panties just as the paper had reported that the first two victims had. However, they had omitted details. The way her body was posed, the bruises on her torso and neck, the bugs nibbling at her flesh.

"What is her name?" she asked softly.

"Judy Benson," Detective Cortez said. "We found her purse over there behind those oaks. She's twenty-two, lives in an apartment in town."

A commotion sounded behind her, and Captain Black cleared his throat. "It's the press. I'll take care of it. Stay here, Cortez."

The air stirred with humidity, made hotter by the tension humming between her and Cortez. A fly buzzed around her face, and she swallowed back bile at the acrid smell of the decomposing corpse.

Determined to hold herself together until she was alone, she honed in on the visual details of the crime scene. His MO, his choice of the underwear as a killing tool, the way he'd left the body exposed, all were signs that would help her get inside the killer's mind and create a profile.

The perpetrator had spread the girl's legs as if to suggest a sexual crime, but he'd folded her hands together as if she was saying a prayer and laid them across her bare breasts. Maybe he was conflicted?

A prayer or was she supposed to be asking for forgiveness? Maybe she was supposed to be worshipping him? "Was she raped?"

"We won't know for sure until the ME gets her on the table. With the other two, there were indications of sexual intercourse, but not clear signs of rape. Sex could have been consensual but something snapped with the guy and he killed her."

"Or he may have killed her during sex—some men can only achieve sexual satisfaction through violence," Jenny said. "Were the other two girls posed like this? Legs spread, hands folded?"

"Identically."

She tucked a strand of hair behind one ear. "How long was she missing before you found her?"

"Her roommate said she disappeared Thursday night after happy hour from a bar on River Street."

"And the other girls?"

"The first victim, Dodie Tinsley, a waitress, disappeared after work one night. She was found two days later. The second girl, Penny Ann Wayling, was last seen at the Java Monkey where she was supposed to meet a date. A coed discovered her body the next day while jogging."

Jenny angled her head. "Any leads so far?"

He shook his head, his jaw tight. "We've interviewed old boyfriends, roommates, neighbors, friends. And we're checking their computers for e-mails, chat rooms, to see if the girls might have tried one of the online dating services. But so far we don't have any viable suspects."

"How about the underwear? Did it belong to the victims or did he bring it?"

"He brought it. We think he took the victims' as a trophy."

"I see. Did he always use black?"

Raul nodded. "We're trying to trace where he purchased them."

Jenny pushed to her feet, needing to escape. The girl's sightless eyes screamed for help and were tormenting her. The cops would have pictures of all the crime scenes. She'd review them, compare them, see if she noticed anything else.

The detective cleared his throat. "Now what can you tell us, *Dr.* Madden?"

Again he said the word *doctor* as if it was a four-letter word.

"Listen, Detective Cortez," she said, facing him. "I don't know if you're always this rude, or if you've just decided to grace me with your bad attitude, but I didn't ask to be here today. So if you don't want my help, that's fine. I can leave now."

She started up the path, trembling as she tried to escape the awful smell and the image of that poor girl lying so hopelessly dead. Because no matter what she or he did, they couldn't bring her back.

And she didn't intend to show her grief for the victim to this cold-hearted bastard.

RAUL WANTED to let her go. But Black was approaching with a scowl on his face, and he knew he'd better shape up.

"Captain Black requested you come, so he'll want to hear what you have to say."

Her eyes blazed, and she hesitated. "And you, Detective?"

He couldn't lie. "You like sexual deviants. I have trouble with that."

"Like?" she said, her voice dripping with sarcasm. "If that's how your thought processes work, then you like criminals."

His eyes glittered with disdain. "I hunt them down and put them behind bars to get justice."

"And I treat sexual deviants to alter their negative behavior."

"They don't deserve to be coddled or to be released on some stupid insanity plea."

"Maybe, maybe not. But they're human, and if I can help one of them, keep one from committing a crime, from killing an innocent person or themselves, then I've saved a life, and that makes my job worthwhile."

Captain Black strode toward them, his jaw set in granite. "Dr. Madden, is there a problem here?"

She turned her gaze toward him, and Raul scowled. Let her run to his boss, whining that he'd insulted her pride.

"No," she said instead. "I was just coming to relay my initial assessment."

Black shot Raul a dark look. "Good. We need *all* the help we can get on this case."

She nodded, a sheen of perspiration glistening on her face. "All right. Given the way the body has been posed, it suggests a sexual predator."

"Even though the girls weren't obviously raped?" Black asked.

She nodded. "Yes, perhaps he sees them as sexual beings, but he thinks they're dirty girls and wants to expose them for what he perceives they are. He also may be conflicted. He likes them, is tempted by them but blames them for his fall from grace so he shames them. Ultimately, he has to kill them so they won't entice him or any more men."

"That makes sense," Black said. "Go on."

"Your killer is probably in his early twenties. He may have suffered a psychotic break meaning his reality is altered. Skewed. He's attractive, appeals to young girls, or else he wouldn't be able to approach them and convince them to go with him. He looks trustworthy, like a nice guy." She exhaled shakily and Raul realized she wasn't as cool as she'd acted. The girl's death had disturbed her.

"Although he appears confident," she continued, "he's

an underachiever. He might have been abused or neglected when he was young or picked on by other kids. Maybe he's been overlooked at work, passed up for promotions or works at a job that's below his intelligence, a menial job he feels is beneath him. He craves power and control."

Raul studied her earnest expression, knew she believed the hogwash she was saying. "What good does all this do us? It doesn't tell us who our killer is."

Her gaze was steady, unfaltering. "If you understand how the perpetrator thinks, get into his head and understand his motivation, you can use it to weed out suspects."

"I am in his head," Raul shot back. "He's a sick sadistic monster who takes young women's lives. Now I need evidence, clues that will show me where to find him or where he'll strike next."

Jenny sighed. "If you learn more or want to share details with me, let me know. The more information I have about the victims and the crimes, the more I can fine-tune the profile."

"Right," Raul said, although he didn't hide his contempt.

Black cleared his throat and sent Raul a sharp look, but she actually offered him a smile. A condescending smile that knifed through him as sharply as her comment about family had.

"You have my number," she said, then headed up the path to her car.

Raul tried not to admire her body or the fact that she'd stood her ground when he'd cut her down.

"You're a piece of work, you know that, Cortez," Black growled.

He shrugged. "I tell it like I see it."

"I asked Dr. Madden here on a consult," he continued,

pissed, "and I don't expect you to undermine my authority by implying that she's incompetent."

"You know how I feel about shrinks," he said between clenched teeth. "We don't need her."

"Maybe you *do* need her," Black said. "You're letting your past and your emotions cloud your judgment."

"That's bull."

"Is it?" Black arched his dark brows. "You're too wrapped up in your bitterness, and blaming every shrink in the world for your wife's death, that it blinds you to the fact that Jenny Madden might be of value to our case." He paused, but barged on before Raul could argue, "You haven't dealt with your wife's death yet, Cortez. You need help."

"The only thing I need is to be left alone so I can do my job."

Black pinched his fingers together, then parted them a fraction of an inch. "You're this far from being suspended pending a psychiatric evaluation, Cortez. Either straighten up your attitude yourself or you're off the case."

Anger heated Raul's blood. "You wouldn't do that."

"Try me." Black narrowed his eyes. "Maybe Jenny Madden is just the person you should see. And on a professional basis. I could make that happen."

"Over my dead body."

"Then prove you don't need counseling by working with her." Black folded his arms. "Show her the respect she deserves. She might teach you a thing or two. She knows the mind of the sexual predator better than anyone around."

He bit back a caustic remark, and fisted his hands by his side.

"After you finish here, and interview the family, then

take copies of the files on the other vics to Dr. Madden. Let her study them and see what she says."

Raul silently cursed but nodded. He couldn't disobey a direct order.

Not when it meant his job.

Besides, he could handle one little Jenny Madden. He could always pretend he was accepting her help. But he didn't have to like it. And he sure as hell wouldn't let her get inside *his* head or pour out his heart to her.

After all, that heart had died the day he'd lost his wife and child. And it was dead forever.

JENNY ROLLED her shoulders to alleviate the tension knotting the muscles as she climbed into her car and started the engine. It was only midafternoon, and she'd already had a hell of a day. The visits with her mother always drained her, but she normally took a long run afterward to relieve the stress.

Not today. No, she'd had to endure Raul Cortez, a man with a mountain of an attitude and dark eyes that were sinfully sexy, but haunted by some demons that only he knew. Because he obviously wasn't a sharing kind of guy.

But dealing with the detective was nothing compared to the anguish she'd felt at the sight of Judy Benson's dead body. An innocent girl who'd died before her time.

Nothing she or Raul Cortez could do would bring her back.

Tears burned her eyelids, but she waited until she was driving away before she let them fall. She'd cry now, and then she'd focus on work.

Finding the girl's killer and giving her justice would ease the pain of the family. She'd dealt with enough victims to know that. So she would help, regardless of how much it hurt her to see the family and friends suffering.

She'd even tolerate the surly detective for Judy Benson's sake.

The wind tossed her ponytail around her face, and she pushed it back. Her stomach growled, reminding her she hadn't eaten since breakfast, but the scent of the girl's corpse lingered on her skin, and her appetite vanished.

With a sigh, she made the turn to her place, knowing she had to shower before she could stomach food. When her cell phone rang, she checked the number, half expecting it to be the hospital. Sometimes her mother became agitated after she left and she had to return, or the nurses had to give her extra medication. Instead it was Captain Black.

"Dr. Madden speaking."

"Dr. Madden, this is Adam Black."

"Yes?"

"I want to apologize for my detective today. He can come across as being rude, but he's a good cop. One of the best I have and totally dedicated to the job."

"No problem."

"Good. Because I—we at the department—value your expertise and I'd hate for his behavior to dissuade you from assisting us."

"Trust me, Captain, my skin is thicker than that. Working with him won't be a problem."

His sigh reverberated with relief. "I'm glad to hear that."

"So it's my job, not me personally?"

A long hesitation. "I really can't say any more. If Raul wants to tell you, well, he should explain himself."

Curiosity nibbled at her, but she refrained from asking more. She wasn't sure she wanted to know the reason for the man's brusqueness. It was probably best that they agreed to dislike each other and leave it at that.

"He's going to drop by later with the victims' files. Maybe you can pick up something we missed."

Great. She'd get to see the man twice in one day. She couldn't wait. "That's fine. I'll be home all afternoon. Tell him to stop by anytime."

He thanked her and hung up, and Jenny spun down the road to her new home, an old Victorian she was in the process of renovating. She loved the unique architecture, but it needed a face-lift, and paint. A work in progress, it would be something she could see visible progress more quickly than her patients.

Pushing aside her frustration, she parked and dragged her weary body inside. A shower, a salad and glass of wine later, she felt more relaxed.

But knowing Detective Cortez would stop by kept her on edge. Curiosity nagged at her. If she was forced to work with Raul Cortez, she needed to know all she could about the man.

Fortified by that thought, she decided to research him online. A quick search revealed his father was Cuban, his mother American; they'd met after his father had escaped into the country, married and had five children. They lived in Miami where Raul had resided until two years ago. He had served with the Miami Dade Police Department until his wife had been murdered.

His wife and unborn child.

A lump lodged in her throat, but she forced herself to read on: Louie Mulstein had been arrested for butchering his family in cold blood. The therapist who'd evaluated the perpetrator stated that he was schizophrenic and off his medication, but that she had stabilized him and that he was no longer a threat. House arrest and an ankle bracelet would suffice until the trial in which the defense attorney would be pleading an insanity charge. Raul Cortez had argued, insisting the man was dangerous and shouldn't receive bail.

But the judge had rendered his decision and released the man according to the guidelines recommended by the court-appointed therapist.

That night Mulstein had escaped and butchered Raul's wife, who was pregnant with his child.

Raul had found the man still in his house, bloody knife in his hand, and the man had attacked him. Raul had shot him, killing him instantly.

But it had been too late for his family.

Her throat closed as she studied the photo of the detective at the graveyard. It was a cold, windy, rainy day, and his massive shoulders were hunched in grief. His expression appeared tortured as he lay a bouquet of roses on the freshly turned grave.

Her comment today, her dig that he wasn't a family man, echoed in her mind, and she dropped her face into her hands with a pained moan. No wonder he had reacted to her with such fervor.

She'd made a beginner's mistake. Had allowed the man's insulting attitude to push her buttons on a personal level, and she'd struck back.

Why? Because she'd just come from her mother's and felt like a failure because she helped others but couldn't help the one person in her life who mattered most.

Her reasons, excuses, didn't matter. She was a professional and she would act like one. Raul Cortez deserved her sympathy and understanding, not her disdain.

Maybe he did blame the therapist, even her, but his grief was eating him alive. And Jenny understood grief. Although technically her mother was still alive, she'd mourned her loss for years.

Unbidden came the image of Judy Benson's pale, stiff body and those haunting eyes. The detective would have to relay the news to the parents. Then the nightmare of their sorrow would begin.

And the questions. Who would have done such a horrible thing to their daughter?

Maybe she should look at her files to see if any of her prior or current patients fit the profile.

Immediately two names sprang to mind—could one of them be the strangler?

Damn Jenny.

Dr. Rupert Zovall closed his eyes, envisioning Marilyn Madden's pale face as she lay propped against the hospital pillows when he'd last seen her in Charleston. He'd treated Jenny's mother for years, had been her psychiatrist since her breakdown.

Why the hell had Jenny moved her mother to that Coastal Island Research Park in Georgia? Hours away from him in Charleston?

Because she thought Marilyn needed another doctor? Thought the psychiatrists at CIRP could do something for her that Rupert hadn't been able to do? Thought he was incompetent?

Hell, he'd been her lifeline back to reality in the few lucid moments she'd experienced.

Another image rolled through his head; this one from years ago before…before he'd lost her that day. She had been so young and beautiful, a vision of loveliness that had robbed his breath at times. He'd known it was taboo to fall for a patient, but he had fallen hard.

Then her husband had interfered.

But at least when she was in Charleston, he could monitor her daily.

Bolstered by the fear creeping through his veins, he carefully packed his toiletry bag, then placed it by the door beside his computer bag and suitcase. His palms were clammy as he wrote a check and left it for the maid service, then he flung his computer bag over one shoulder, stacked the toiletry bag on top of his rolling suitcase, and headed outside to his Mercedes.

He had to get to Savannah. Had to see Marilyn Madden before she started ranting crazy things and aroused curiosity. Before the doctors messed with her medication.

Before anyone discovered their secret and started asking questions.

Chapter Three

"Mrs. Benson, I'm so sorry for your loss."

Raul patted the woman's knotted hands and waited for the dam to break. It did a second later, and she burst into tears.

Her quiet demeanor reminded him of his mother, and a pang of guilt hit him that he hadn't talked to his family in weeks, hardly at all since his wife had died.

He folded the fragile woman into his arms and let her cry her anguish and shock. Though Judy had been missing for days, her mother had held out hope until the end. Most families did.

Until they received the final word that their loved one was dead.

Finally Judy's mother's sobs settled into a low sniffle, and she wiped at her face. He handed her a handkerchief and allowed her a moment to dry her eyes.

"Do you know who killed her?" she asked in a tortured whisper.

"I'm afraid not, not yet." He inhaled and forged on. "I promise you I will find the guy, Mrs. Benson."

She nodded, although grief strained her features. "I...I don't know what to do now." She gave him a helpless look, and he squeezed her hands.

"You have some time. Is there any other family you want to call?"

"My sister, I suppose. Judy's dad...he died a few years ago. And there's no other children.

"Did you talk to her roommate?" Mrs. Benson asked. "Did she know who Judy went out with that night?"

"We did talk to her," he said quietly. "But she said she left the bar before Judy. She had a test the next morning, but Judy wanted to stay."

"She shouldn't have left her alone," Mrs. Benson murmured.

"No, and she's beating herself up over that," he said. She'd been practically incoherent with guilt when he'd first interrogated her.

Her expression turned contrite. "I...I guess that was a mean thing to say."

He smiled. "You're grieving, Mrs. Benson. It's allowed."

A small smile broke through her grief, then, as if she remembered the circumstances, immediately wiped it off.

"It will be a couple of days before the medical examiner releases Judy's body," he said. "During that time, you can talk to your sister, start making arrangements."

She nodded, and more tears trickled down her cheek. "There's so much to do...." Her gaze lifted to his. "You'll let me know when you find the monster who did this?"

"Absolutely. Now I'll have an officer take you wherever you want to go." He guided her to the door, watching as she slowly wove her way through the precinct beside the officer.

His promise to find the killer echoed in his head, and he strode out the door and headed back to the bar where Judy had last been seen. He'd questioned everyone there before, but he'd do so again. Then he'd beat the streets for a witness as to who she'd hooked up with that night.

Maybe he'd find a clue, and he wouldn't have to drop those files off at Dr. Madden's.

JENNY BREWED a pot of coffee, then accessed her work files and skimmed through them.

She had several seriously disturbed patients, and two weekly group therapy sessions—the first, a group of obsessive-compulsives; the second, a group of sex addicts. She combed through the members of the sex addicts group, but nothing stuck out as suspicious. One man was addicted to porn, and had sought therapy because his boss had threatened to fire him for viewing it at work. One female was a nymphomaniac, one man was obsessed with having sex in public, and two others had various fetishes.

Moving on, she looked through the other patient files, studying the notes she'd taken during their private sessions. Two names tickled her conscience.

Clyde Anson and Jamal Rakely.

Clyde was a masochist and had been forced into therapy by the courts for assaulting a woman. His preference toward asphyxiation sex made her uneasy—the killer had strangled his victims. He fit the profile in other ways, as well—he was in his mid-twenties, had been raised in an overly religious home by an overbearing mother and had been abused.

Jamal Rakely also raised her suspicion. During a domestic incident he'd turned violent, had lost control and strangled his wife, but his attorney had pled him out on an insanity charge. His history: Jamal had witnessed his father murder his mother when he was five.

Her cell phone rang, and she startled, sloshing coffee on her skirt. She yelped, grabbed a napkin and dabbed at it, then jumped up and retrieved the phone. A check of the caller ID box showed Dr. Solaris, her mother's doctor at CIRP. A knot tightened in her stomach.

"Dr. Solaris, this is Jenny Madden."

"Hi, Jenny. You visited your mother this morning?"

"Yes, I always do on Sunday. Is she all right?"

"Yes, she's resting now."

Jenny frowned. "Are you sure? Sometimes after I visit she becomes agitated."

"Actually she's been sleeping all afternoon. But the reason I called is that I've phoned Dr. Zovall several times requesting he fax me your mother's files, and he hasn't sent them yet. Have you spoken with him recently?"

That was odd. "No, but I can give him a call. Have you tried his cell number?"

"Yes. I've left messages. Anyway, he's probably tied up with another patient, but I wanted you to know that I'm going to proceed and conduct a full and extensive evaluation this week. It'll include a gambit of tests, complete blood work, tests for physiological conditions, chemical imbalances, MRI, cat scans and neurological tests."

"Good. I expected you would want to conduct your own tests. And frankly, after all these years and her lack of progress, I think it's time."

"You voiced your concerns to Dr. Zovall?"

"Yes."

"I don't imagine he was happy about you pulling her from his treatment."

"No, not at first. But he cares for my mother and wants what's best for her, so he finally agreed that she should see someone else. I think he feels guilty for her lack of progress."

A noise outside jarred her, and she peeked out the window but saw nothing suspicious. Antsy, she walked through the den to the kitchen and checked the back door. A stray cat slithered through the yard, jumped on the trash can and the lid rattled.

Sighing, she silently chided herself.

"I'll call you when we learn the results."

"Good. And if you need me at any time, you have my number." She hesitated. "I understand this change may be unsettling for Mom."

"Don't worry," Dr. Solaris said. "I'll take good care of her. We have some new treatments that are working well with other patients. Hopefully your mother will respond positively, as well."

"I hope so, Doctor."

She hung up the phone, but another noise out back startled her, and when she glanced through the window her heart raced. A man was skulking across the backyard, his face hidden in the shadows.

FRUSTRATION TIGHTENED every nerve in Raul's body as he parked in front of Dr. Madden's house. He'd spent hours requestioning everyone in the bars along River Street and turned up nothing. No one remembered Judy Benson. No one had seen her abduction.

Scrubbing a hand over his bleary eyes, he studied the doctor's house. Evening shades of gray cloaked her blue Victorian. The traditional lines, and the fact that it needed painting and new shutters shook his preconceived image—he'd expected her to own one of the new modern lofts or a mansion on Skidaway Island, not this fixer-upper.

Not that he gave a damn. The less he knew about the woman the better. He'd just drop off these files and leave her to them. Then he'd grab a beer and a pizza and develop a plan to trap this strangler before he struck again.

He climbed from his car and eased up the sidewalk, scanning the periphery of the house and yard. A shadow slithered between the tall oaks in back, moving toward a side entrance.

The strangler case on his mind, his instincts soared to life. He removed his gun from his shoulder holster, and eased around the side, crouching down to hide behind the bushes as he approached. A scraggly haired young man stood on tiptoe and peered in the window.

A Peeping Tom or could this be the killer? Maybe he'd been watching the crime scene and followed Dr. Madden home.

Anxiety made his hands sweat, but he closed the distance, careful to tread lightly.

A twig snapped, and the lurker spun around.

"Police, put your hands in the air where I can see them."

"Wait! Don't shoot," the guy cried.

"Hands up now, buddy." Raul inched closer, senses alert as the young man's hands shot into the air.

He was about twenty-five. Light-brown hair that needed a cut, eyes that looked glassy as if he might be high. Around five-eleven, medium build, scruffy.

"It's not what you think," the young man screeched. "My name is Bailey."

"It's exactly what I think," Raul snapped. "You're skulking around this house looking for a way to break in, and I'm going to arrest you."

"No, I swear. This is my sister's house." His expression turned panicked. "Jenny Madden, she lives here. I'm her brother."

Raul narrowed his eyes. He didn't see any resemblance. "If you were her brother, why are you sneaking around? Why not knock on the door like a civilized human?"

Bailey glanced around nervously. "I wanted to make sure she was alone, that I didn't barge in on company."

Raul reached for his cuffs. "Right. Turn around and spread them."

Bailey puffed up his scrawny chest. "Ask her, you jerk! Jenny will tell you."

He wasn't about to open the door until this guy was subdued. "Big mistake calling a cop names." Raul spun him around, then snapped the cuffs on his wrists.

Bailey jerked against the restraints and yelled an obscenity. "Jenny!"

The back door suddenly eased open, and Jenny Madden poked her head out.

Bailey stamped his foot. "Jenny, tell this SOB who I am."

Her expression registered concern but also irritation as she stepped outside. "You can release him, Detective Cortez. That's my brother, Bailey."

Raul growled. "You're kidding?"

She shook her head, her lips pressing together in a thin line. "No, it's true. He's harmless, really."

Raul hesitated. He wanted to run the guy in for being an a-hole, but he was already skating on thin ice with the doctor and his captain, so he uncuffed him. "Don't let me catch you sneaking around anyone's house again, even if it is your sister's."

Bailey gave him a murderous look, but he was obviously shaken. He started to say something, but Dr. Madden held up a warning hand. "That's enough, Bailey. Go inside. *Now.*"

Her tone brooked no argument and her brother showed his first sign of intelligence by ducking inside.

"Sorry about that," Raul said. "With a killer on the loose, and him sneaking around—"

"Understandable," she said quietly.

He nodded, and they stared at each for a long moment, his pulse pounding at the way the moonlight glowed off her silky hair. She looked tired and vulnerable and for a moment as if she needed comfort. And those lips…kissable pink lips if he'd ever seen any.

Damn it. He did not like this woman, and he sure as hell didn't want to be attracted to her.

Yanking himself back in control, he cleared his throat. "I stopped by to drop off those files. I'll get them." Without another word, he rushed to his car and retrieved the files. She was still waiting on the stoop when he returned, a slight breeze tossing the strands of her hair in disarray.

"Thanks." She ran a hand over her forehead as if she had a headache. Probably due to that smart-assed little brother.

Not that he gave a damn about Jenny Madden's private life or problems. "Well, I'll let you go visit with your brother." Still, he didn't move to leave. Wondered suddenly why her eyes looked red as if she'd been crying.

"I'll study the files tonight," she said, "and try to get back with you tomorrow."

He nodded, waiting to see if she offered anything more, but tension hung in the air between them.

Finally she arched a brow. "Is there something else, Detective Cortez?"

He had no idea why he hadn't left yet, but that smarmy little brother of hers disturbed him.

A second later disgust filled him. She was a shrink, for God's sake. And her brother was none of his business,

Schooling his thoughts, he handed her his business card. "Call me when you're ready to talk."

An odd look flickered across her face, then she gave him a clipped nod and shut the door in his face.

But as he strode back to the car, an uneasy feeling gripped his stomach. Bailey Madden was young, a smart-mouth, but surely he wasn't dangerous, was he?

Yet Jenny Madden had looked tense, worried, shaken. Was she afraid of her brother?

Chapter Four

Humiliation stung Jenny's cheeks as Detective Cortez strode to his car, and she spun around, hands on hips to face her brother. Today had been hell, and now he had been skulking around her backyard like a thief in the night. No wonder the detective had handcuffed him.

She tried to keep her private life separate from her business yet Bailey was the thorn in her side. As soon as the thought came, guilt suffused her. He was her little brother, had suffered more than she had when their father had walked out. He'd desperately needed a man in his life.

"What do you want, Bailey?"

He shrugged, his black T-shirt emblazoned with a crude comment about women, stretching across his chest. "What makes you think I want something? Maybe I just came to visit my big sister."

"Yeah, and you have some great property to sell me, too." Impatience sharpened her words. "Come on, Bailey. Spill it. Are you in trouble again?"

A sheepish look he'd used on her all her life graced his face. She'd vowed not to fall for it again. "Don't play coy. What happened? Did you get arrested? Have you been gambling? Doing drugs again?"

"I just need a loan, Jenny." He jammed his hands in his pockets and turned them inside out. "See, just some cash to get me by."

"I'm not giving you money to buy drugs."

"But I need food."

"Get a job like everyone else." She paced to the bar in the den and poured herself a glass of wine. "I need repairs done. If you're interested, I'll pay you for work."

"Dammit, Jenny." He slumped onto the sofa. "I got an offer back in Charleston. It's warehouse work but it pays well."

As long as it was legitimate work, she didn't care what he did. "But if you worked here, you could see Mom."

He vaulted off the sofa, bouncing on the heels of his sneakers. "Why should I visit her? She doesn't even recognize me when I do, much less hear what I say."

"She does hear you," Jenny insisted. "I know she's trapped inside, listening and trying to cry out. We just have to keep reaching out to her."

He threw up his hands, nostrils flaring. "How fair is that? You help her but not me."

"I've helped you before, Bailey, but it's time you help yourself." She sipped the glass of wine. "I've had a hell of a day, and work to do. Now if you won't visit Mom, then you should leave."

"You bitch!" He stalked toward her and grabbed her wrist, twisting it painfully. "You can't leave me hanging like this. I…owe some people."

She wrenched her arm free. Bailey had never gotten violent before, but his behavior seemed to be growing more erratic. "Get out, Bailey. And come back when you can act like a human."

Bailey shot her a murderous look, but a knock sounded

at the door and he jumped back. Jenny froze, and inhaled a deep breath. Who was here now? She hadn't been in Savannah long, didn't know many people.

Trembling, she glanced through the sheers. Detective Cortez stood at the door, feet braced apart, body rigid.

That photo of him at his wife's grave flashed back, and compassion mushroomed in her chest. On the heels of compassion something dangerously akin to attraction zinged through her.

No…she didn't want to be attracted to this man. Not when he had so much baggage. Not when she had problems of her own.

Not when he hated her job and everything she stood for.

RAUL FISTED HIS HANDS by his sides, his temper racing as he waited on Jenny Madden to answer. He'd had a bad feeling about her brother, so he'd sat in his car for a few minutes deciding to make sure everything was all right.

Through the sheer curtain, he'd seen Bailey grab Jenny Madden, and he'd shot out of the car without thinking. No one abused a woman when Raul Cortez was around.

She opened the door, arms folded across her chest, her eyes wary. "Detective Cortez, what are you doing here?"

"I never left," he said curtly.

Her eyes widened. "You were watching me?"

He glanced past her at her brother, who quickly averted his gaze and turned to study the CD collection on the bookcase. "I wanted to see if you were okay."

"I'm fine," she said, although perspiration dotted her forehead and her wrists were red. "My brother and I were just talking."

"It didn't look that way to me."

A soft gasp escaped her. "Trust me, everything is under control."

He stared at her, then brushed past her and grabbed Bailey's arm. "Listen to me, you ever touch your sister like that again, and you won't only end up handcuffed, but you'll find out what it's like to have two broken arms, then cuffs snapped around them."

Dr. Madden gasped again, and Bailey turned white. "I'm out of here, sis. I don't need this crap. Not from you or this jerk."

Raul let him go, and so did Jenny.

But she turned on him, livid. "How dare you barge in here and intrude on my family."

"I've seen plenty of domestic-violence cases, Dr. Madden, and this looked like one to me."

"Then you misread the situation."

He narrowed his eyes, saw a flicker of fear and some other emotion he thought was probably embarrassment in hers. "Did I?"

She clamped her teeth over her bottom lip. "Yes. Believe me, Detective, I've treated enough abused women that I won't let that happen to me. If Bailey pulls that stunt again, I'll call the police and have him arrested."

He studied her, wanted to believe her. And he did. "You want to talk about it?"

"No. I can handle it."

"Like you can handle the maniacs you treat?" Sarcasm laced his voice. "The sexual deviants?"

"Yes."

His anger rose again. "You're crazy for putting your life in jeopardy treating psychos who prey on women."

She jammed her hands on her hips, her cheeks coloring.

"I'm no more crazy for doing my job than you are. You put yourself in danger every day tracking down criminals."

His gaze locked with hers in challenge. "I can take care of myself."

She gave a sardonic laugh. "That's right. You're invincible, aren't you, Detective Cortez? No one can hurt you or anyone you care about because you don't care about anyone."

Her words cut him to the bone. Anita's face flashed in his mind, her eyes wide with shock, the blood pouring from her chest. His baby dead before it had ever had a chance to breathe life.

God help him, he hadn't deserved them. But he'd wanted them with every fiber of his being....

Still, it was his fault they were dead. For that he'd never forgive himself.

Or the shrink who'd let the madman who'd murdered them go free.

JENNY SILENTLY berated herself at the pain that darkened the detective's eyes. Pain she had put there with her careless words.

What in the world was wrong with her? Why did this man push all her buttons? Make her resort to fighting back when they should be working together? When she understood his attitude and had the professional expertise to help him?

Which was the crux of the problem. He didn't want help or anything to do with her. He'd written her off without a chance.

A chance she wanted because in spite of her humiliation over the confrontation with Bailey, and Raul Cortez's disdain for her job, the fact that he'd defended her had touched her.

She always took care of everyone else. Having a white—well, dark—knight charge to her rescue only heightened the insane attraction she felt toward the man.

Too bad he hated her.

"I'm sorry, Detective Cortez, that was out of line. I... went too far."

His cold look made her shiver, his eyes scrutinizing her as if dissecting a bug. "Captain Black told you about my wife, didn't he?"

She chewed her lip again, remembering that haunting photo. Though still broad-jawed and -shouldered, his face was more gaunt now, his cheeks hollow grooves in his sculpted face, lines of anguish creasing his eyes. "Captain Black didn't tell me anything."

"But you dug it up on your own?" He didn't wait for a response. "Quite the resourceful shrink, aren't you?"

"I...Detective...Raul, I only wanted to understand you. You blame the psychiatrist who recommended your wife's killer be set free on insanity charges, don't you?"

"It *was* her fault. If she hadn't convinced the judge to let a maniac go free, my wife would be alive."

"That thinking is not only emotional but irrational. According to your logic, I should blame every cop in the world if one is bad. And now I should blame the police for Judy Benson's death because they failed to catch the killer."

"Maybe we are at fault," he growled. "We're obviously missing something. But to call me irrational? I thought shrinks were understanding, not judgmental."

A heartbeat of silence stretched between them. "I'm not your shrink," she said in a quiet voice. "You, I, doctors and policemen, we're all human. We all make mistakes, we save some, we lose others. Goes with the job."

He gritted his teeth. "I don't need a lecture, Dr. Madden. And you will *never* be my shrink."

"Fine, I'm not asking to be," she snapped. "But if you want to be effective, you have to find a way to let go of your bitterness."

He squared his shoulders, towering over her, furious at her assault. "I do my job fine. But I can't and won't change my opinion about yours."

Her heart ached for him. "You deserve to be happy again, to move on with your life."

"My life ended two years ago," he said in a tortured voice. "I only live to catch psychos like those you protect. And I don't need or want you analyzing me."

Emotions dried her throat. "What *do* you need?" she finally asked.

He stared at her so long she thought he wouldn't answer. The intensity of his gaze sent a shiver of heat rippling through her, jumpstarting a fantasy journey in her mind. His wide angular jaw and that bronzed skin taunted her to touch him. The hum of sensuality radiated off him in waves. He was undoubtedly the biggest, most masculine man she'd ever met, and he had needs, fierce needs that were driving him.

His eyes flickered, turned jet-black. He wanted her.

Not in an emotional way, but his body craved release.

Just as her own begged to be touched. She wanted to see him naked, wanted to allow him to use her to make his pain go away.

God, she must be crazy. She'd never let a man use her….

"A good lay, that's what I want and need," he said with a chilling smile. "But that isn't all. Justice. I want justice for these dead women."

She jutted up her chin. "I would be a good lay," she said, "probably the best you've ever had."

A muscle ticked in his jaw, and he wet his lips with his tongue, drawing her gaze there. Heaven help her, but she wanted to lick his lips. Taste him one time. Make him smile until all that rage dissipated.

Thankfully, self-preservation kicked in. "But I can't, won't sleep with you," she said, mustering conviction to her voice. "As far as your second request, though, finding justice for these victims, I'm completely onboard with that."

His thick eyebrows rose. "Good. And for the record, I don't need your pity. I can get laid whenever I want."

She laughed, a hollow sound that she knew would score a direct hit at his inflated ego. "Right. Glad we got that out of the way. Now, if we're going to work together, we need a truce."

He stomped closer to her, eyes narrowed. "Oh, we're going to work together," he said as if in challenge. Or perhaps his captain had ordered him to do so. "But you are not going to get inside my head, Dr. Madden."

"Jenny," she said, knowing the first step to softening him was to personalize their relationship.

"'Doctor' is fine."

"I can't work with someone who says my title as if it's a four-letter word."

He hissed. "Fine. *Jenny.*"

She had to stand her ground. Lose this battle and she'd be forever cowing to him. "You stormed in here to save me from what you perceived was an abusive situation." She paused, crossing her arms and straightening to her full height. "There's more than one type of abuse, Raul. And you're walking dangerously close to the edge yourself."

She'd struck a direct blow. He actually flinched. Then for the briefest of seconds, remorse softened the cold glint in his eyes, and he scrubbed his hand over his face with such a weary sigh she wanted to retract her words.

Just as she opened her mouth to apologize, he spoke. "You're right," he said, throwing her off balance. "My mother taught me better."

The reference to his mother resurrected memories of her own. The morning, the decision to make a change with her therapy, her mother's empty eyes. The loss…

Pain tightened her chest, and she breathed in deeply, refusing to give an inch. Knowing if she did, she'd never earn this man's respect.

"So let's start over." She offered her hand, and he stared at it as if it was a venomous snake that might bite him. But finally he took it in his. A tingle of anticipation and desire shot through her, but she tamped it down. This man might be potently sexy, desperately in need of some TLC. But his heart was closed, and she didn't intend to get hers broken.

RAUL CLOSED THE DOOR and leaned against it, trying to calm his racing heartbeat as he contemplated what had just happened. Dr. Jenny Madden had gotten to him.

He'd been half out of his mind when he'd seen her brother grab her, and then she'd mentioned his family, and…he'd wanted to run.

But he hadn't. He'd stood there and endured her.

Because for some insane reason he hadn't been able to drag himself away.

Maybe he was crazy. Needed help.

But not from her. Not the woman with those cornflower-blue eyes and those pink lips that she liked to nibble when she got nervous.

And as much as he believed he was right, that a shrink was responsible for his wife's death, a seed of admiration for Jenny Madden had sprouted. She'd been professional today, had handled the crime scene with dignity, and her conjecture about the perp might be dead-on. She'd also stood up to him and her no-account brother.

And that mouth of hers was too tempting. So was that body. And when she'd shaken his hand, a bolt of electricity had sent his blood racing, like it hadn't raced in years.

Gritting his teeth, he forced himself to think of his dead wife. There was no way in hell he'd desecrate her name or his unborn child's by taking a shrink to bed.

HE STUDIED the newspaper photo, his blood sizzling with excitement. Finally he was receiving the attention he deserved. The honor. The respect.

The crime-scene photos didn't reveal the details, though. Didn't show the way he'd left the girl posed for the world to see her ugliness. Didn't show the care he'd taken when he'd made love to her first. The way he'd satisfied her before giving himself release. The way he'd kissed her before he'd left her.

And there was Dr. Jenny Madden bending over the body. The article said the cops had asked for her help.

Laughter bubbled in his chest. They needed a psychiatrist's help to find him. As if that would do any good.

And Dr. Madden…they had no idea they'd played right into his hands. He'd wanted her to notice him, to know he was watching her. That one day he would have her, too.

But not yet.

Because Jenny was sweet. Not like the whores who offered themselves to men in bars. Not like the ones who teased him, then turned away like he wasn't worth their time of day.

But he had found the perfect way to show them that he was the master. Already his body twitched for another.

He could almost feel the satiny softness of her panties as he ripped them down her legs. Feel her insides quiver as he entered her. Hear her cry of pleasure when she came.

Hear her scream as he tied the black lace underwear around her neck and choked the life from her.

Chapter Five

Raul paced his kitchen, unable to sleep. He had notes about the three girls' histories on a corkboard above his desk and the files strewn across it. He'd reviewed the interviews with the first two victims' families and friends, searching for a connection, but had found nothing. No common churches, organizations, groups, chat room visits. They didn't frequent the same stores and neither had complained about boyfriends or ex-lovers hassling them.

Had they been chosen at random? Or was he missing something?

He scrubbed a hand over his face, weary and irritated that he still had Jenny Madden on his mind. Dammit, the woman had infuriated him. She knew about his wife. Had checked into him, for God's sake.

Pain knifed through him. He didn't want her knowing. Didn't want her looking at him with pity or sympathy, or as a pet project that she thought she could save by having him sprawl on her couch and pour out his heart. Pouring out his heart would not bring his wife or child back.

Nothing would.

The emptiness inside him churned with agony, and he

cursed. He wouldn't be caught off guard again. If she knew all about him, he'd find out everything he could about her. After all he was a cop. Maybe Jenny Madden had some secrets in her closet.

Like her brother for one…

Did that little bastard have a record?

Determined to arm himself with the ammunition to protect himself, he entered Jenny Madden's name. He searched the databases for records on her and her brother but found nothing incriminating on Jenny. Not even a damn parking ticket.

Although Bailey Madden popped up with a rap sheet. He'd been arrested for illegal gambling, had a DUI and a misdemeanor drug charge.

Raul drummed his fingers on the desk. Odds were that he was gambling again, desperate for money and that he'd hit his sister up to bail his sorry ass out of trouble.

He hoped Jenny had meant it when she said that if he got rough again, she'd call the police.

He searched further and discovered Jenny had graduated from premed from UGA, then attended Emory Medical College in Atlanta. She had published several papers on sexual deviants, had also studied dissociative identity disorder, and at one time had run a program for young girls with eating disorders. She frequently spoke to women's support groups for abused and displaced women returning to the workforce. Begrudgingly, admiration for her kicked in. His youngest sister had been involved with an abusive man once, and it had taken a family intervention and counseling to convince her to leave.

Jenny had also worked at a private counseling service for two years, but had moved to Savannah to assume the position at the Coastal Island Research Park, CIRP, because she had transferred her mother there for treatment.

He frowned, his interest piqued, and he dug deeper, the personal information he uncovered in a small piece about Jenny for a local press disturbing him on an elemental level. Apparently, her mother suffered manic depression and had slipped into a nearly catatonic state, although there were no details as to the cause.

Was that the reason Jenny had studied medicine, specifically psychiatrics and mental disorders?

BETWEEN THE INSUFFERABLE HEAT, nightmares of the Savannah Strangler sliding a pair of silk panties around her neck, and the image of Raul Cortez's pain-filled eyes haunting her, Jenny barely slept all night. Groggy and exhausted the next morning, she showered and washed her hair, then toweled off. By the time she slugged down a cup of coffee and dressed, the doorbell was ringing.

She raced toward it, knowing she had only a few minutes before her first appointment at the hospital.

Ralph Martin, the forty-something carpenter she'd hired for the renovations, stood at the door. As usual, he wore a baseball cap tugged over a high forehead, and his wavy gray-blond hair was shaggy and pulled into a ponytail at the base of his neck. He'd already repaired the roof, re-stained the molding in the dining area, painted the upstairs and was ready to start on the lower level. Once the work was complete, she planned to install a security system.

He shuffled in, leaning heavily on his uninjured leg. Sympathy for the man welled in her chest. She hadn't asked what had happened, although he'd claimed it was an old war injury.

"Morning, ma'am."

"Good morning." She lifted her hair off her neck and clipped it into a twist. "The air-conditioning is on the blink. Can you take a look at it?"

He nodded and went to his truck for a flashlight and tools, and she grabbed her purse and laptop. Ten minutes later at CIRP, she checked in with her receptionist.

"Good heavens, did you see this?" Renee gestured toward the paper. "There was another murder yesterday."

Jenny paused by Renee's desk and glanced down at the headline. The Savannah Strangler Strikes Again.

Her heart clenched as she remembered the horror of the crime scene. "Yes, as a matter of fact, the police called me in to work up a profile. They'll probably be back. Please remember to be discreet about our patients."

Renee gaped up at her. "Dr. Madden, I'm not a gossip."

"I didn't mean to imply that," Jenny said softly. "It's just that the police might be feeling desperate and may push for information on my patients."

"Oh, I see." Renee smiled, her hurt feelings soothed. "Of course I'll refrain from comment."

Jenny thanked her, grabbed a cup of coffee, went into her office and reviewed her schedule. A few minutes later the group filed in. She arranged the chairs in a circle and greeted each of her patients, offering coffee or water as they took seats. As she expected, though, some of the members looked nervous while others openly checked out the individuals.

"I'd like to welcome you and remind you that anything discussed in this group is held in the strictest of confidence." She reiterated that they had signed contracts not to discuss each other's problems or personal issues with outsiders.

"I understand opening up in a group is difficult, but over time we'll learn to trust each other and offer support." She laid down a few ground rules regarding the safety contract they had signed stating they wouldn't harm themselves or anyone else. If so, she had to warn that person. She also reminded them of boundaries, to respect each other's personal space, that touching another member was allowed only if the person gave permission. "Each of you is here to explore your individual problems—"

"You mean our addictions," Kylie Wells said with a grin.

Jenny smiled in return. "Yes. But we're not here to criticize or belittle others. And there is to be no sexual contact with each other outside the group."

"Why not?" Carl Huggins asked.

"Because that would defeat the purpose. We're here to talk, nothing more. If you have relations with one another, then it breaks the trust of the group."

The two women nodded although Carl still didn't look convinced. And Stan Leys, a heavyset balding guy, kept staring at her shoes. He had a foot fetish.

"Why don't we start by getting to know each other? Tell us your name, your likes, anything you want to share about yourself."

The group shifted slightly, sharing a nervous look, then Kylie spoke up again. The girl wasn't shy.

"I'm Kylie Wells, and I like sex." Another toothy grin and she tossed her long black hair over her shoulder. Although attractive, Jenny sensed that underneath, Kylie suffered from low self-esteem. "I like sex. A lot of it." She crossed her legs. "I'm a nymphomaniac."

"I like sex, too," the curvaceous redhead, Annika, said.

"Especially in public." She ran her long fingers over her pencil skirt seductively. "I like to be watched."

Will Cane cleared his throat. "I'd like to watch you sometime."

Jenny gave him a stern look. "Please remember the ground rules."

"What's wrong with liking to be watched?" Annika arched a brow. "Don't you have fantasies, Dr. Madden?"

"There's nothing wrong with having sexual fantasies, even playing some of them out, within reason of course." She tried to gentle her voice. "But we can't allow those obsessions to destroy our relationships with others, threaten our jobs or endanger ourselves or others. We need to ask ourselves if we're trying to fill a void with meaningless encounters or experiences when there's a more deep-seated issue at hand."

"I feel pretty damn happy when I'm having sex, and looking at naked women," Will said.

"Sex can definitely spike your endorphins. But, Will, your obsession is jeopardizing your job. You have to learn boundaries, set limits, control your actions." She turned to the member who hadn't spoken yet. "Now let's move on. Carl, would you like to share?"

Carl narrowed ice-green eyes, eyes that sparkled with invitation. "I like bondage." He removed a silk scarf from his pocket. "And my conquests must wear satin and silk."

"I like satin and silk," Annika said softly. "That doesn't seem like a problem at all."

Jenny arched a brow. "Carl, why don't you tell them the rest?"

Carl smiled, revealing even white teeth set in his tanned face. He was attractive and he knew it, but could be devious, too. "I like to take prisoners," he said. "Keep my women locked up for days. I force them to walk around in nothing but satin panties all day, to be ready for sex at my beck and call."

Kylie was practically panting and the other men leaned forward, obviously turned on, as well. "What happens if they refuse you?" Kylie asked.

"I punish them." Carl wound the scarf tightly around his fist. "Punish them so they know never to disobey me again."

Jenny stared at his hands, the way he flexed the scarf. His obsession with satin and silk.

Could Carl be the Savannah Strangler?

RAUL TACKED PHOTOS of all the victims on the whiteboard, then listed details about each girl below it, still searching for a connection. But nothing jumped out, except that all the women were in their twenties. All pretty.

All dead at the hands of the same man.

According to Jenny Madden, the killer was also in his twenties. Probably attractive enough to convince the girls to go with him.

Unless he'd drugged them with an injection or by spiking a drink.

He pulled up the autopsy reports and studied them. Due to the nature of the crime, the M.E. had specifically checked for date rape drugs—Rohypnol, GHB or Ketamine Hydrochlorine. Rohypnol had been found in Judy's body, which would explain why she had put up very little fight, although not in the first two victims. But that didn't mean the killer hadn't used it—it was only detectable within seventy-two hours after being used, and those two victims had been dead longer than that when their bodies had been discovered.

The killer must have taken the girls to a remote location since so far no one had reported anything suspicious on the designated dates. He'd obviously used a condom so they hadn't found fluids for tracing. And according to the report, he had bathed them after sex. Traces of bleach had been discovered on their skin—he'd wanted to destroy any evidence he might have left.

Then he'd carried them to the woods and left them exposed.

But he'd covered his tracks so they had only a partial footprint which looked as if it had come from a man's boot.

Forensics had turned up very little except for a splinter beneath Dodie Tinsley's fingernails. They were analyzing it now. Maybe it would eventually lead to something, but it was a needle in a haystack.

Dammit. Someone had to have seen or heard *something*. He'd beat down the streets until he found a clue.

Securing his weapon in his shoulder holster, he tugged on his jacket and headed outside to his car. Traffic was fairly light for tourist season, and he made it to River Street in record time. Sightseers mingled with the locals, strolling along the river, pushing baby strollers and walking dogs.

He entered a gift shop selling homemade taffy and souvenirs and showed the photos of each victim to the clerk and owner but neither recognized them.

He continued combing the shops and restaurants, talking to owners and waitstaff. Two people recognized Judy Benson from the newspaper article, but not in person. Finally he entered the pub where Judy had been last seen at happy hour.

A girl with blond streaks in her spiked black hair asked for his order, but he declined. Her face blanched white when he showed her the photo.

"I did see her that night," she said. "Aaron over there waited on her."

Aaron was the bartender with the lizard tattoo and the nose ring. Midmorning the bar was fairly empty, only a couple of truckers eating burgers and having a beer. Raul slapped Judy's picture on the bar.

"You waited on this woman the night she died?"

The young guy's gaze skated to the photo, and he sloshed beer over the mug he had just filled as he set it on the bar. "Yeah. So. I wait on a lot of people."

Defensive jerk. "What do you remember about her?"

Aaron shrugged bony shoulders. "She was hot. Ordered a cosmo."

Raul nodded. "How many?"

Another shrug. "A couple."

Raul's jaw snapped tight. "Did you spike her drink?"

Aaron took a step back. "Her drink was spiked? The paper didn't mention that."

"Did you do it?"

"No. Hell no. I could get fired for that."

"How did she pay? Was she buying her own drinks?"

"I don't remember."

"Listen," Raul growled. "It may not seem important, but anything you can tell us might help."

"She paid cash for the first drink, but a man sprang for the second."

Now they were onto something. "What did he look like?"

Aaron scrubbed the spilled beer with a drying cloth. "Light hair. Short, maybe military cut."

What if he was a soldier on leave? Maybe from one of the naval ships? He might be here today, gone tomorrow before they discovered his identity.

"Did he give you cash or a card?"

"A card I think."

"Dig through and see if you can find it."

Aaron nodded. "I'll have to ask the manager to pull up last week's receipts."

"I'll wait."

"He's not here right now," Aaron said. "Doesn't come in until four, then closes."

Raul silently cursed. "All right. Ask him to find it, then give me a call." He tossed down his business card. "Keep an eye out for him again. If he comes in, let me know."

"Sure."

"Oh, and you could watch out for guys spiking girls' drinks."

The bartender fidgeted. "Look, man, I can't keep my eye on every customer all the time."

Raul glared at him. "Maybe not, but try. If this girl's drink hadn't been spiked, she might not have left with this murderer. Then she'd still be alive."

He strode out and walked to his car, but his cell phone rang as he climbed in.

Wiping sweat from his brow, he connected the call. "Cortez."

"Hey," his partner said. "I ran a check on the databases for similar cases to the Strangler, and for escaped mental patients, parolees, prior crimes involving sex offenders in the area."

"Yeah, any hits?"

"Two. Guy named Clyde Anson. History of sexual abuse and violence. Court ordered him to seek therapy."

"And the second?"

"Jamal Rakely. Strangled his wife after sex, but got off on an insanity plea."

Raul's mind raced. "They both live in Savannah."

"Yeah, and get this. Both are enrolled in treatment programs through CIRP."

"Don't tell me that Dr. Madden is their psychiatrist?"

"How'd you guess?"

Raul clenched his jaw. He'd confront Jenny and find out what she knew about the men. They might have two viable suspects now.

JENNY MASSAGED her temple as the group filed out. Getting them to admit that they had a problem was a start. Understanding the difference between normal behavior and addiction would take time.

She filed the tape of the session, along with her notes, then pulled the file on her next patient, Clyde Anson, when Renee buzzed her.

"Dr. Madden, Detective Cortez is here to see you."

Jenny sighed and checked her watch. "Send him in."

She smoothed down a strand of hair that had escaped her twist, stood and met Raul as he opened the door. Angry dark eyes, a sculpted face, a scar along his brow, a five-o'clock shadow and it was barely lunch—he looked tired and troubled, as if he'd been up all night. And so handsome that something low and sensual streaked through her abdomen. She wanted to soothe his stern brow. To stroke the tension from his rigid shoulders. And wipe the scowl off his face.

"Dr. Madden—"

"Jenny," she reminded him softly.

His jaw tightened. "I have some questions for you."

She gestured toward one of the two wing chairs facing her desk, then walked to her office chair and sat down.

"We ran a check on sexual deviants and criminals in the area, and surprise, surprise. Two of your patients' names popped up."

Jenny glanced down at the file on her desk. Before he even told her the names, she knew who he was referring to.

"You know I can't discuss my patients with you, Raul. That would violate patient-doctor confidentiality."

He slapped Judy Benson's photograph in front of her. "We're talking about murder, Jenny. Three so far."

"I'm well aware of that. I was at the crime scene, remember?"

"And you know that this guy is going to kill again."

She did know that. And she wanted to stop him, too. Didn't want any victims' deaths on her head. But she still had her ethics. If she lost her integrity, what did she have left?

Raul reached out, pressed his hand over hers. His voice was gruff when he spoke. "If one of these men is the killer, Jenny, you can't protect him."

The truth of his statement warred with her own anguish for the dead girls. "I know that, too. But unless I have reason to believe that one of my patients is a serious threat to himself or others, or that he has committed a crime, I can't discuss their personal sessions."

Raul wrapped his long, blunt fingers around hers and stared at her, emotions she couldn't discern blazing in his eyes. "These men are dangerous, Jenny."

She drew in a calming breath. "I'm very aware of that, Raul. I know what I'm doing."

"Do you?" His voice dropped to a lethally low tone. "You fit the MO of his targeted victims, Jenny. What if he comes after you?"

Chapter Six

Anger churned through Raul. He didn't know what had possessed him, but the very idea that Jenny Madden would protect a killer at her own expense infuriated him.

Was the woman a damn fool? Did she think she could save the world? What drove her to try to do such a thing?

The truth hit him square in the gut. She was trying to save others because her mother was ill.

Maybe he and Dr. Madden were more alike than he'd originally thought. He wanted to protect others, especially the women and children who couldn't protect themselves. But he'd failed, and he felt as if he'd have to atone for his failures the rest of his life.

"Jenny, please," he softened his voice, hating that he felt anything at all when anger had been his only friend for so long. He latched on to it again. "Don't put yourself on the line here. We need you to tell us what you know about these men."

She stared at him for a long moment, not batting an eye at the way his tone had hardened again. Instead her fingers curled inside his palm.

A strange feeling tightened his belly. He suddenly

imagined meeting her at another time. Not on a case, but over a drink or dinner. On a beach with the breeze tearing her silky hair out of that sophisticated knot at her neck and running his fingers through it. When life might be different, free of violence and the threat of crazies preying on women and destroying lives.

Hell, what was he thinking? His wife had died at the hands of a madman because of a do-gooder like her.

"I understand what's at stake, Raul," she said in a low voice. "I'm asking you to trust me. I'm a professional." Her breathing vibrated in the tension-filled air between them. "If I learn that one of my patients is the man you're looking for, I will turn him in. Until then…" Her smile was sad but her voice full of conviction. "Until then my hands are tied. If my patients can't trust me with their confidence, I can't help them at all."

He worked his mouth from side to side, studying her. Wishing she'd bend. Admiring the fact that she didn't.

And despising himself for liking her.

But hell, he didn't want to find her in the woods with a pair of panties wrapped around her neck.

Another dead woman on his conscience was more than he could stand.

He pulled his hand away, folded his arms. "I'll question these guys with or without your help. And if you know something and don't come forward, I'll charge you, too."

Her gaze met his, steady, a silent moment passing between them that he didn't want to explore. Finally she spoke. "Do what you have to do, Raul. And so will I."

He gave a clipped nod, knowing that legally she was right, that he couldn't force her to divulge confidential information. But he didn't like it one damn bit.

Without another word, he stalked from her office. But he'd be back with more questions. Maybe with a warrant if he found something concrete on one of her patients.

JENNY LEANED BACK in her chair and closed her eyes, breathing deeply to calm the raging emotions stirring in her chest. She didn't understand why Raul Cortez affected her so, but her knees had been knocking and her hands trembling as he'd stared at her with his intimidating eyes.

She'd been threatened before, with bodily harm and lewd sexual comments, and had learned to cope and not to react, not to be goaded. But Raul's dark intensity and the power of his rage and determination assaulted her on a deeper level.

He wasn't driven by a mental illness or the desire to hurt others, but by the need for justice for the victims he tried so hard to protect. By the anguish in his soul over the loss of his own wife and child.

She wanted to assuage his pain, to help him find this killer and put him away, yet her own convictions kept her rooted to the spot and silent.

How could she feel something for a man who hated everything she stood for? Who thought that by providing therapy for violent offenders and sexual predators she was somehow aiding their cause?

The image of Judy Benson's face flashed into her head, and guilt niggled at her. Could one of her patients be the Strangler? Carl, the man in her group session with the fetish for silk and satin?

He liked power, enjoyed exerting control over his conquests. She'd requested each group member keep a daily journal of their thoughts and behavior. If she found proof that he was hurting women, she'd dismiss herself from his care and turn him in for questioning. Just as she would any patient she suspected might harm himself or others.

Her intercom buzzed, and she punched the connect button, knowing she had to get on with her day. Couldn't dwell on Raul Cortez or the pain in his voice and eyes.

"Dr. Madden, your next appointment is here."

She glanced at her appointment book and mentally composed herself. Thankfully Raul had already left. It wouldn't do for Clyde Anson to see the police at her door.

She stood, brushed down her skirt, checked her jacket to make sure it was buttoned, had to look professional.

As soon as she opened the door, the big man stalked in, six-two, two hundred pounds of muscle screaming a bad attitude. "Hey, there, Doc," he said with a lopsided grin.

With high cheekbones, a broad jaw, harsh eyes, and a body like a linebacker's, Jenny had to admit Clyde was nice looking, could even be charming. But a devious nature lay beneath his smile.

He was also a masochist and had the scars on his body to prove it. He'd carried his sexual fantasies too far twice and a woman had nearly died. The judge had forced him to seek therapy, and he pretended to play the game, but she didn't trust that he was sincerely dedicated to rehabilitation.

His gaze fell to the newspaper article on her desk, and his mouth widened into a full-fledged grin.

A chill skated up Jenny's back. He fit the profile of the killer.

She gestured toward the chairs flanking her desk.

"Ladies first," he said in a deep voice.

Jenny claimed one of the chairs, angling her body to face him. He sat across from her, leaned back as if relaxed, draping one bulky arm across the back of the chair.

Memories of his file sprang to mind—the images of the pictures of the woman he had sadistically beaten. His comments about the twisted games he liked to play.

"What is it, Doc?" His eyes twinkled. "You look uptight this morning."

Knowing he was baiting her, she schooled her reaction. "I'm fine." She reminded him of the safety contract and confidentiality issues.

"I got your rules, Doc," he said with a leer. "Hands off the iceberg doc, right?"

"Respecting a person's personal space is one step in exercising control over your actions," she said in response. "Physical contact is not appropriate to our relationship. We're here to talk about your problems. Now, where would you like to start?"

"I could tell you about the girl I laid last night." She didn't allow smoking in her office, but still he removed a pack of cigarettes, tapped them on his thigh, then slid one between his fingers and rolled it around. "She tasted like sugar and spice and everything nice." He hesitated and leaned toward her with a cocky look in his eyes.

"Is your relationship with her merely sexual or have you dated her before?"

"We hooked up in a club," he said. "Man, she had on this hot little black skirt and a top that dipped down to her navel." He whistled. "Thought I'd lose it just looking at her twitch her butt on the dance floor."

"So you danced?"

He chuckled. "Yeah, she rubbed herself all over me."

"You liked her?"

"I liked the way she stripped."

Jenny maintained a steady look. He was testing to see

if she'd blush or become embarrassed. But he had no idea the comments she'd heard from other patients, and this man wasn't going to rattle her.

"She liked it rough, Doc. Liked it when I tied her up. Liked it when I blindfolded her and made her beg for me to stop."

"Did she tell you that?"

"Yeah, she told me to go harder and faster. It was part of the game," he said. "She wanted it bad. She panted my name, begged me to hurt her."

He balled his hand into a fist, crushing the cigarette in his palm. "So I did."

Inside, Jenny tensed, but she stared at him deadpan.

Had his masochist behavior led him to be a cold-hearted killer?

RAUL FORCED IMAGES of Jenny from his mind as he climbed in his car and punched in Keegan's number.

"Keegan, anything new on the case?"

"Some bartender you talked to phoned with the credit card number and name you asked for."

"Yeah?"

"Guy's name is Bobby Machete. Haven't been able to locate him yet."

"Keep looking." Maybe Keegan would turn up something. "Do you have addresses and places of employment for Clyde Anson and Jamal Rakely?"

"Yeah, hang on a minute. I'll pull up the info."

Raul pulled out his pocket notebook and grabbed a pen, ready to take down the addresses and phone numbers.

"Anson rented an apartment in town, and works as a bouncer at that new club, Universal Joint." He recited Anson's home address, phone number and contact information for his parole officer. "Rakely works at the fish house down at the docks. He's renting a place on Tybee.

"Do you want me to meet you to question them?" Keegan asked.

"No, I can handle it. I'll fill you in when I'm finished."

Keegan hung up and Raul punched in Anson's home phone number, but received no reply. If he worked at a club, he probably wouldn't report until later. He tried Rakely's home but again got nothing, so he headed toward the docks. Traffic was thick with tourists and locals, and the late-afternoon sun nearly blinded him as he parked at the marina. Shrimp boats coasted in, the shrimpers dragging nets up to empty them into the vats they used to collect their day's catches.

Normally the ocean and ships relaxed him, but the heat intensified the strong scent of fish and left a ripe stench in the air, the smell growing pungent as he approached the fish house where the fish were sorted, packed and stored for transporting to restaurants and stores. A long shack open to the public held fresh market seafood, so he stepped into it, searching for Jamal Rakely.

A robust but haggard-looking woman wearing a grimy apron stood behind a cooler display of assorted seafood. In the workroom behind her, Raul spotted a large man gutting fish.

He stepped up to the counter and identified himself. "I need to speak to Jamal Rakely."

The door squeaked as two customers came in, and she glanced nervously at him then the customers. "Listen, is he in trouble? 'Cause we're trying to give him a chance, but I don't need no trouble."

"I just want to ask him some questions, ma'am. It won't take long."

She gave him a wary look. "All right. But can you take it outside?"

He nodded.

Wiping her hands on her apron, she turned and yelled through the opening. "Jamal, someone here to see you."

The big man turned, eyes glinting with questions in his light-brown face, a cleaver in his hand. When he saw Raul, his lips converged into a firm line of anger, but he dropped the knife, then stalked through the swinging door. He, too, wore a grimy apron, the stench of fish guts rolling off him.

Raul gestured toward the door. "Let's step outside, Mr. Rakely."

Rakely cut his eyes toward the woman. "Tamara, I'll be right back."

She nodded, and he pushed through the door, his wide shoulders stiff, sweat dripping down his neck. Scars criss-crossed his beefy arms, another long one down the side of his right cheek. Probably prison earned. Then again, maybe he'd earned them on the streets.

"What's this about?" Rakely asked, arms crossed over his massive chest. "I've been to see my parole officer on time."

Raul shrugged. "Your name came up in an investigation I'm running. Where were you Saturday night, say around midnight?"

Rakely frowned. "Got off work around ten. Went home and watched the tube."

"Alone?"

His eyes narrowed to slits. "Yes. Why you asking?"

"A woman was murdered that night. Judy Benson. You know her?"

"No." A sarcastic chuckle escaped him as he gestured toward the fish house. "Not unless she works here."

"Ever been to the pub on River Street?"

"I stop in for a burger sometimes. But drinking is against my probation."

"And you're staying clean?"

The guy waved a hand over his apron. "Yeah, clean as it gets."

The man the bartender described definitely didn't fit this guy's description. But still, he had a history of violence, had strangled his own wife.

He removed the photo of the other victims. "You know either of these women?"

Rakely studied the photos, a smile quirking his lips. "Good-looking chicks. I wouldn't mind knowing them."

Raul clenched his jaw. "They were both murdered."

Rakely stiffened, then paced across the dock, the wooden boards creaking with his weight. "I knew this would happen," he snarled. "A guy has a record, and every time some petty crime occurs, you'll be all over my tail."

"This wasn't a petty crime, Rakely. These girls were strangled. That fits your MO."

Rakely grinned, showing off a gold tooth. "Didn't you hear? I was let out because of mental defect. Not guilty, the jury said."

"I'm not buying the plea," Raul growled. "You look like you're pretty sane to me."

Rakely threw his head back and laughed. "Hell, that's because this shrink is making me all better. Giving me some pills to take. Letting me cry on her couch." He glanced at the photo again, then his face contorted with a stony look that hinted at pure meanness. "And she is pretty.

Just like these girls. She could make all my problems go away if she'd let me take her to bed."

Anger surged through Raul. Every male sexual deviant in Savannah probably thought the same thing. And he was sure some of them tried.

Trust her, she'd said.

Trusting her wasn't the issue. This man outweighed her by over a hundred and fifty pounds, could force her to do God knows what. And she dealt with sickos like him all the time.

A vile expression darkened Rakely's cold eyes. "Now, if you're done with me, I got fish to gut." He took one last look at the picture. "Better watch out, though. With Dr. Madden helping you, it's bound to tick off this guy. She might end up dead like those girls."

NIGHT PAINTED THE ROOM in shadows just the way he liked it. The brunette lay beneath him, tied to the bed. A little chubby for his tastes but it meant she had big breasts and enough of a butt to hold in his hands. Enough to pad her as he drove himself deeper into her flesh.

She had been so easy to seduce. Shy. Needed attention. Really a sweet girl.

Not like the others.

Or so he'd thought at first.

But once he stripped her and began to suck her breasts she'd begged him to love her.

Her cries of pleasure had spurred his own, and he'd barely rolled on the condom in time. But he had, and his secrets would be safe.

She gazed up at him, her lips swollen from his mouth, her body quaking from the orgasm he'd given her. He enjoyed giving them pleasure before he put them to death.

"Please, again," she pleaded.

He shook his head no. The voices were already starting in his head. Telling him she was a bad girl. That he was bad for screwing her.

In his mind, time lapsed. Memories assaulted him.

The beating would come soon. The incessant scrubbing of his skin to cleanse him of his sins. The bleach to wash away the stench.

The endless prayers.

He slid the pair of silk panties from beneath the mattress where he'd buried them when he'd first brought her to his bed. Her eyes widened in confusion, then she bucked and tried to move but he had her tied good. He had all his supplies ready. The bleach. The plastic to carry her in. The spot chosen to dump her body. This time he'd throw off the cops. Instead of the woods, he'd take her to the marsh.

Slowly he wrapped the panties around her neck and began to squeeze.

Chapter Seven

By the time Jenny finished with her last patient, recorded her notes for the day and detailed strategies for the group session and individual patients, dusk had come and gone and night had set in. Renee had long ago left for home. Jenny shut down her computer and locked her files.

Her session with Clyde Anson had disturbed her. She'd studied his body language and had to ask about his encounter with the woman. Specifically if she'd been alive when he'd left her.

He'd thrown his head back and laughed, then said she'd been alive and begging for more.

Always alert to the possibility of a patient with an ax to grind or lurking around, she locked the door behind her and checked the halls for stragglers. The security guard on her floor stood by the elevator and threw up his hand. Relief skated through her, making her realize she was on edge because of the Strangler stalking the town.

Her cell phone rang as she reached the elevator, and she slid it from her purse and checked the call. Dr. Solaris's office.

Taking a deep breath, she answered the call. "Dr. Madden speaking."

"Jenny, it's Payden, Dr. Solaris's secretary. He asked me to call and tell you that your mother had a bad day."

"What happened?"

"He's not sure. He ran some tests and wanted to talk to you about them. Said maybe you could stop by. Then he went to check on her and she started screaming and ranting incoherently."

"I'll be right there." Rolling her shoulders to alleviate the tension, she punched the elevator button, stepped inside and hit the button for the fifth floor. As soon as she stepped off, she sensed the agitation on the wing. Heart racing, she bolted to the nurse's station.

"Dr. Madden. I need to see Dr. Solaris."

"He's with your mother right now, Doctor. You can wait."

"No, let me go. Maybe I can calm her or figure out what set her off."

She wove through the corridor, past a male nurse who had just exited her mother's room. He looked frazzled and fresh scratch marks marred his arms and neck.

Jenny pushed open the door and paused, cataloging the scene in her mind. Like a rerun she'd seen a dozen times, her mother was screaming at the top of her lungs, throwing her fists and kicking, struggling to escape. "You can't keep me here. He found me, he hurt me again. Don't let him come back and get me!"

"Marilyn, no one is here to hurt you," Dr. Solaris said quietly. "We're here to help you recover."

"He's all over me, he's here. I see him in the corners, hiding to get me when you go."

Pain swelled in Jenny's chest, and she bit back tears as her mother sobbed hysterically and continued to fight.

Two female nurses held her down while Dr. Solaris tapped a hypodermic and jammed it into her mother's arm.

He glanced at her as he finished with a grave sigh. "I don't know what triggered her attack, but she's been screaming that we have to release her for half an hour."

"Delusional again," Jenny concluded as she mentally played various episodes over the years.

"Let me go! Please don't hurt me!" her mother cried.

Jenny slowly approached, wanting desperately to calm her mother, but knowing the meds had to kick in. "Has anyone been in her room?" she asked.

The nurse shook his head. "No, just the staff. We changed shifts at three."

She explained to the doctor that she thought the male nurse had been the trigger, that her mother didn't like to be touched by men. She'd even wondered if she'd been sexually abused as a child, but Dr. Zovall hadn't determined that was true.

Her mother slowly calmed, and Jenny slid a hand over her mother's. Over the years her skin had grown drier, and now a few age spots discolored the surface. "I'm here now, Mom. It's going to be all right. I promise."

"Don't let them hurt me anymore," her mother cried. "Please make them stop."

"I will," she said softly. "Don't worry. Dr. Solaris and I are going to protect you."

For a moment her mother seemed lucid and she squeezed Jenny's hand. Jenny's hopes soared that perhaps Dr. Solaris would heal her mother. Then the medication must have kicked in—she closed her eyes and drifted to sleep.

Dr. Solaris frowned over his bifocals, dismissed the nurses, then urged her to step into the hallway. "I wanted to talk to you about the tests I ran, Jenny. I don't want to disparage your mother's former doctor, but he was over-medicating her."

She angled her head toward him. "You're certain?"

"Yes. I'm going to wean her from the heavy narcotics and streamline her medications. It's possible that the combination is causing more problems than they're solving. That is, with your permission of course."

"I brought her here because nothing has worked so far," Jenny said. "I've read your work, Dr. Solaris. I trust your judgment."

"Good. I'll start weaning her from the meds immediately." He excused himself, and she joined her mother again.

For a long time she simply sat and stared at her sleeping form, struggling to remember a time when her mother had been well, when they'd shared simple pleasures like baking cookies or shopping, but the memories were so few and far between that they seemed nonexistent. Weary, she lay her head down on the edge of the bed. She wanted her mother to get better, but sometimes she feared she'd lost her forever.

That she would always be alone.

Raul's face popped into her head, and her stomach tightened. But she quickly banished the image. Nothing was going to happen between her and the detective because he hated what she did.

And she couldn't do anything else because giving up her belief that she could help people meant giving up on her mother. And she refused to do that no matter how many of these episodes she endured.

Besides, the detective's job was dangerous. He lived on the edge, might or might not come home at night. She wanted a settle-down kind of man, one who would never leave her.

She stayed with her mother for another hour, but finally accepted that she wouldn't wake until morning, dragged herself from the chair and left for home. Heat suffused her as she stepped outside, and her stomach growled. She drove the short distance to her house, grateful the carpenter had left for the day. A salad and then sleep. God, she wanted sleep and to be left alone.

But as she walked up to her porch, the silhouette of a man lurked in the shadows.

This guy was big and brawny. Raul?

Her breath caught, and she paused at the foot of the steps. Not Raul.

Jamal Rakely. He was pacing like a caged animal, his anger vibrating in the click of his hard soles on the slatted wooden porch.

How had he found out where she lived? And why had he shown up tonight?

RAUL DROVE to the bar where Clyde Anson worked, the Universal Joint, a place that had once been a gas station but which had been converted. It offered a great patio along with a DJ and dance floor and was a popular hook-up spot.

The place was dark, smoky, and pulsing music flowed through the sound system and spilled outside. Only a few lone patrons combed the bar, some sitting outside for quesadillas and burgers and beer. He checked out the inside and saw a lone female or two. Didn't they realize they were endangering themselves by hooking up in bars?

The press coverage should have been enough to frighten them.

He went straight to the bar. "I'm looking for Clyde Anson."

The skinny college-aged kid shrugged. "His night off."

He gestured around the nearly empty room. "As you can see, Monday nights are slow."

Which meant the man could be home. Or anywhere in town.

He flashed the pictures of the three victims, but the guy denied seeing any of them in the bar. So did the few waitresses.

Irritated, Raul left and drove toward the address Keegan had given him, then parked. He hadn't liked Jamal Rakely and had ranked him high on his suspect list. He definitely wanted to talk to Anson first hand. But when he strode up to Anson's door and knocked, no one answered.

He peered through the front window. It was dark, no light on, no movement at all. He circled around back and checked through the sliding glass doors. No light in the kitchen, no signs of anyone inside. He jiggled the door, hoping it was unlocked, so he could slip inside. No such luck.

But moonlight illuminated the kitchen table and he spotted several newspapers on the table, specifically the ones describing the girls' murders. The three victims' faces stared up at him, mocking him to go inside.

For a moment, he considered breaking in and searching the guy's house, but anything he found would be inadmissible in court and if—no *when*—he caught the Strangler, he wanted to make sure he stayed behind bars, wasn't released on a technicality.

Frustration knotted his shoulders but he forced himself to walk away, back to his car. He'd have to visit Anson tomorrow, find out where he'd been.

A few minutes later he grabbed a pizza and took it back to his place, a duplex he'd rented on Tybee because he wanted the fresh air and beach access although he couldn't quite afford the beachfront property. But he liked to jog along the shore, feel the salt air spray his face.

He dropped the pizza onto the rickety table that came with the place, changed into running shorts and a T-shirt, then headed outside. Moonlight streaked the beach as he jogged along the edge of the water, the sound of the ocean roaring in his ears drowning out the voices in his head, the screams of his dying wife praying that he'd save her before it was too late, the cries of his child who'd never been born or had a chance at life.

Tormented by their loss, he pushed himself harder and harder until he could think of nothing but putting one foot in front of the other and shutting out the sounds.

Yet Anita's face melded with the three victims of the strangler, and he couldn't run fast enough or far enough to escape them.

Panting and sweating, he finally jogged back the other way, save a few late-evening walkers, having the beach to himself. By the time he reached the duplex, he was exhausted and needing food. He let himself in, took a quick shower and wolfed down the pizza along with a beer.

The second bedroom served as a home office, and he had copies of the case and photos tacked to a board above the desk. He made a note of his encounter with Jamal Rakely, then finally flopped down on his bed. His dead wife's picture stared at him from the nightstand, her eyes haunting him as he tried to go to sleep.

But when he closed his eyes, another woman's face floated into his dreams. Jenny Madden's.

For a moment pain receded and other thoughts replaced them, stirring the blood in his loins. That long, blond hair flowing over her back and into his hands. Her supple breasts spilling over white lace. Her mouth begging him for a kiss, her spreading her legs to take him inside.

In the midst of the fantasy, a gavel struck down. The sound of it rocked him from his sleep, thrusting him back to the day the judge had released Mulstein because that shrink had advised him to. The grotesque images of death followed. The blood pooling around his wife's body as she lay dead in his arms.

The determination in Jenny's eyes when she'd refused to talk to him about her patients. The lust and sick need for violence in Rakely's eyes when he'd referred to Jenny.

Cursing, he rolled over and pounded the pillow. He could not lust after her. Could not get involved with her or care about another woman. Not only would he put her in danger because of his job, but she dealt with psychos and sexual deviants every day. It was only a matter of time before one of them came after her.

And if he cared, he'd be around to watch her get hurt. Possibly die.

He couldn't live through that kind of pain again.

JENNY FROZE, pulse racing. A patient showing up at her home definitely violated her contract with him. But if she backed down, showed fear, and called the police without talking to him, she'd lose the patient's respect, so she'd hold off until she at least knew the reason for his visit.

Still, her training kicked in, along with self-preservation, and she reached inside her purse, and retrieved her phone in case she needed to call for help.

He stopped pacing when he saw her, although anger radiated off him as he met her on the top step.

"What are you doing here, Jamal? You know this is against the rules."

"I saw your name in the paper at that crime scene. You sent that damn cop to me, didn't you, you bitch?"

Jenny sucked in a breath. "I did no such thing, Jamal. And I need for you to calm down and refrain from calling me names."

His nostrils flared as he pushed his face into hers. She inhaled, smelling his fury but not alcohol, thank God. When he drank he became violent, the combination intensifying his bipolar disorder.

"You said to trust you, that you'd help me stay out of jail," Rakely snarled. "But you gave me up."

Jenny jutted up her chin. "Listen to me, Jamal. I did not give you up. I was called as a consultant on that case to offer a general profile of the killer. I do not, nor have I ever, divulged privileged patient information."

A long tense second passed, the air vibrating with the sound of his anger. "Then how did he get my name? And why did he show up at my job?" Frustration edged his voice. "You know how hard it was for me to land work, and here I am gutting fish to pay the damn rent and I may lose that lowlife job now."

Jenny's heart squeezed. It was a common problem for ex-cons. The obstacles in starting a new life often drove them back to the life they were trying hard to leave.

"Again, Jamal, I would never divulge information on a patient. The police have databases listing prior convictions similar to cases they're investigating. Your name probably came up, and the interrogation was just routine."

She pushed past him to her door, then turned, needing to take charge. "Now, go home. Mind your own business, and keep yourself clean. And don't show up here again, or I will be forced to report you."

He caught her arm, his fingers digging into his skin. "Don't lie to me, Doc. Or you'll be sorry."

She glared at his hand where he gripped her. "Don't touch me again, Jamal, or show up at my home or so will you."

Knowing she had to remain strong, she flung off his hand, jammed the key into her lock, rushed inside, slammed the door and locked it, kicking the dead bolt in as well.

Her heart racing, she sagged against the door, breathing raggedly. Technically, Jamal had just threatened her. She should transfer him to another doctor.

Or report him to Raul.

Then Raul would gloat that he was right about her incompetence, or that her job wasn't worthwhile.

Questions pingponged in her head. What if he was right, and she was wrong?

What if Jamal hurt someone else? What if he was the Strangler, and he had simply wanted to intimidate her so she would call the cops off his tail?

If he killed again, it would be her fault.

Chapter Eight

Jenny had finally settled down after her confrontation with Jamal Rakely, and crawled into bed when a pounding on the door made her jerk her head up. Dear God. Surely Rakely hadn't returned, not after her warning.

Maybe Raul with news of the case. Maybe he'd caught the killer and the women of Savannah could relax.

She slipped on a robe, tying it as she hurried down the steps. Thankfully Ralph had repaired the air-conditioning today and the house had cooled, although instantly her nerves shot up when she peeked through the peephole in the door and saw her brother lurking on the front porch.

Bracing herself for an argument, she unlocked the door, yet she didn't invite him in. "Bailey, it's late. What are you doing here?"

He shouldered his way inside, went straight to the bar and poured himself a whiskey. When he turned to her, she noticed his hands were trembling.

Worry knotted her stomach, but she folded her arms to keep from going to him. She'd rescued him all his life. It had to stop or he'd never grow up. "What's wrong now?"

His eyes flashed with anger at her impatient tone. At least he was coherent enough to notice. "I need a favor."

"I told you, I'm not giving you more money."

"It's not money," he barked. "But if anyone asks, tell them that I was with you Saturday night."

Jenny clenched her hands. He wanted an alibi? "Why would someone ask about your whereabouts?"

He sipped the whiskey. "Just do it, okay?"

"Not until you explain the reason, Bailey. Where *were* you Saturday night?"

He paced to the window, stared out, then turned to her, fidgeting, antsy, panic in his eyes. "At a bar. I got sloshed."

"So what did you do? Hit on somebody's wife or something?"

"No." He shook his glass, ice clinking. "I met that girl in the paper. That dead one, Judy Benson."

A sick feeling clutched Jenny's stomach. "You hooked up with her the night she died?"

"No, not exactly."

Jenny threw up a warning hand. "Stop, Bailey. If you know something about this woman that could help the police find her killer, then you have to go to the authorities."

"I won't talk to the police," he screeched. "But you're helping that pig. He already has it in for me, and if he finds out I met that dead girl at that bar, he'll try to pin her murder on me."

"There's a serial killer preying on women," Jenny cried. "This is your chance to do something good, Bailey. Maybe you saw the killer in that bar. Maybe you can help ID the killer."

She reached for the phone to call Raul, but Bailey

grabbed her arm, gripping it painfully. "You wouldn't call the cops on your own brother, would you?"

"Let me go," Jenny said through gritted teeth.

He tightened his grip, shaking his head wildly. "I didn't do anything wrong, sis. I swear. I didn't hurt that girl. Just don't tell the cops I met her."

"If you didn't do anything wrong, then you shouldn't mind answering their questions."

"But I don't have an alibi for the rest of the night. I passed out in my car. But that pig won't believe me."

Confusion and anger melded in her mind. "I won't lie for you," Jenny said. "You need to step up and be a man, Bailey."

"You and Mom are just alike. You both turn on your family." He threw the empty highball glass against the wall, and glass shattered, raining down.

She flinched, but didn't dare reach for him. "What do you mean by that?"

"Ask Mom," he hissed. "She's the reason Dad left. The tramp drove him away."

Disgust and bitterness hardened his voice, and he pushed her away from him, then stomped out the door, slamming it so hard the pictures on the walls rattled.

Jenny rubbed her arm, her emotions in a tailspin. Why did he blame her mother for her father leaving? And why had he called her a tramp? Her mother had loved her father, had fallen apart when he'd deserted her.

And why was Bailey so worried the police would try to pin Judy Benson's murder on him? Did he have a guilty conscience about something?

She started to reach for the phone to call Raul, but hesitated. Bailey had been volatile, out of control lately.

But he wouldn't actually kill a woman, would he?

RAUL HADN'T been able to sleep and had been reviewing the files when the phone rang—4:00 a.m.

This couldn't be good.

Quickly grabbing the handset, he connected the call. "Cortez."

"It's Black. We have another victim."

Damn. "Where?"

"The marsh on Skidaway. Some old-timers were crabbing and stumbled onto the body."

Raul shoved his bulk off the bed and headed toward the bathroom. "I'll be right there."

"Bring Dr. Madden, too. I want her opinion on why he chose a different spot to dump the body. Or if we might have a copycat on our hands."

Black gave him the coordinates, and Raul splashed cold water on his face, then tugged on jeans and a shirt, along with his boots. On the drive to Jenny's, he grabbed two cups of coffee at an all-night diner and slugged his down.

When he arrived at Jenny's and saw the dark house, he realized he should have called and given her warning, but it was too late now.

Hoping it wouldn't take her long to dress, he hurried to her door and rang the doorbell. He tapped his boot while he waited, and rang the bell again, but still no answer. Finally he pounded on the door.

A light flipped on upstairs, and a second later the door opened, and Jenny appeared.

"Good heavens, Raul, I thought you were Bailey."

His jaw clenched. "He's been hassling you again?"

As if she realized her slip, she bit down on her lip. She looked sleepy and sexy, her beautiful long, blond hair tousled, instantly eliciting fantasies of running his hands through it and taking her back to bed.

He'd much rather be sating himself with sex than processing another crime scene.

Good God. What in the hell was wrong with him? He was not going to take Jenny Madden to bed.

She seemed to recover before he did, although she looked tired, and troubled by something. Probably another confrontation with her loser brother. His gaze skated over her, searching for injuries, for bruises at her wrists.

"What are you doing here, Raul?"

"There's been another murder," he said dragging his gaze back to her face. "I'm on my way to the crime scene. Captain Black wants you to come, too."

Sorrow filled her expression. For a second, regret flamed his conscience. He hated to drag her from her comfortable bed, especially to slog through the marsh and look at a gruesome murder.

"If you don't want to go, I'll tell him," he said.

She brushed her hair back from her face, and his gaze flew to the slender column of her throat. To the flesh exposed as her robe gaped open at her breasts.

Coming here without calling had been a bad idea. A very bad idea.

"No, just give me a minute to throw on some clothes." She gestured toward the foyer. "Wait inside. It won't take me long."

He clenched his hands by his side as she turned and rushed up the stairs. He paced the entryway, trying to put a lid on his surging libido. Instead an image of Jenny stripping came unbidden to his mind. She had supple curves beneath that robe. High full breasts. Nipples a rosy color.

A slender waist and flat stomach. And the triangle of hair at the juncture of her thighs would be golden blond just like the tousled strands on the pillow. Her satiny soft skin would beg for his mouth. And he'd run his hands over every inch of her bare flesh.

Anger at himself surfaced and he put a stronghold on his thoughts as she appeared at the top of the steps and jogged down. She had thrown on a pale-pink T-shirt and jeans that hugged her body, and pulled her hair back into a ponytail. Without makeup, she looked young and vulnerable.

She grabbed her purse and threw it over her shoulder. "Let's go."

Again admiration for her stirred. She seemed to accept whatever he'd asked her to do without complaining. He opened the car door for her outside, then went around to the driver's side, got in and handed her the coffee.

"Thank you, Raul," she said softly.

"You're thanking me for dragging you out of bed to go to a crime scene."

She chuckled. "No, for the coffee. I'm an addict."

Something else they had in common. But he refrained from comment and they drove to the marsh in silence. When they arrived, she didn't wait for him to come around and open the door but opened it and got out. Anita had always expected him to assist her, had wanted him to baby her because her father had spoiled her rotten.

Jenny didn't seem to expect to be coddled or taken care of, which, for some odd reason, tugged at his masculine instincts. Knowing that her father had left long ago, that her brother was a loser and her mother mentally ill, he guessed she'd never had the luxury.

"Is the MO the same?" she asked.

"Black didn't fill me in. I guess we'll see for ourselves."

Black's car and Keegan's were parked on the side of the road, and a crime-scene van rolled up, the team jumping out with their equipment. Black would have called the medical examiner, but at least news of the murder hadn't yet reached the press, so they'd be spared the drill.

"This is different," Jenny said as they walked through the tall sea oats and marsh. "He dumped the other girls in the woods."

Raul nodded. "It made Black wonder if this is the same guy or a copycat."

They spotted the body a few feet away and grew silent. A slightly chubby brunette lay with her hands folded beneath her breasts, her legs spread wide, a pair of black silk panties tied around her throat.

"The position of the body and method of death appear the same," Raul said. "Then why change the dumping ground?"

"He's growing bolder, playing with you," Jenny suggested. "It took longer to find the bodies in the woods. Now he *wants* you to find them. He likes the attention." Her voice quivered. "He's escalating. He won't only kill again, but more often. The good thing about that is that he may rush and make a mistake."

"Let's hope he makes that mistake soon and we can use it to catch him."

As they approached the body, Jenny suddenly gasped, her face paling.

"Oh, my god." She staggered against Raul.

"What is it?" Raul asked.

A low cry escaped her. "I…I know her, Raul." She turned to him, tears filling her eyes. "Her name is Eleanor

Stevens. She's a nurse at CIRP. She works on the psychiatric ward where my mother is staying."

JENNY'S HEART SQUEEZED with emotions. Poor Eleanor. She was only twenty-three, had just graduated from nursing school and come to work for CIRP. She was friendly, patient, easygoing and excited about helping others.

And now she was dead.

The unfairness of it made her double over.

Raul cradled her in his arms, shielding her face as he angled her away from the scene. "I'll take you back to the car. Have someone drive you home."

She clutched him, needing his strength to help pull herself together. Odd but she never leaned on anyone.

But on top of her mother's outbursts the night before, Jamal Rakely showing up at her door and her argument with Bailey, this young girl's senseless death was too much.

He coached her toward the car, but she shook her head, wiping her eyes. "No, I can stay. I'm sorry…the shock just took me off guard."

He stroked her back gently. "It's okay to get upset, Jenny. You knew her…."

"Who found her?" she asked.

"Two old-timers out crabbing." He gestured toward two gray-haired men standing to the side talking to Detective Keegan. Both looked shaken and pale.

"She was a good girl, Raul. She didn't deserve to be left like this." Her mind raced, switched into analytical mode. "I don't understand how he's choosing his victims. The largest percentage of serial killers target hookers. Eleanor definitely wasn't working the streets. She was shy, looking for marriage and kids and happily ever after."

He frowned. "As far as we know, none of the girls were prostitutes or promiscuous."

"He hates women in general," Jenny said. "He must have been abused severely as a child. He feels incompetent. And the only way he feels powerful is by preying on women."

Raul nodded and glanced up as the medical examiner lumbered toward them. He saw Black and Keegan watching him, as well.

"I need to talk to the captain. Tell him we have an ID."

Jenny swiped at her tears, angry at herself for falling apart, but grateful Raul hadn't judged her. "I'll talk to him, tell him what I know about her."

Reluctantly she pulled out of his embrace, swallowed hard as they closed the distance to Eleanor's body.

Keegan was taking statements from the crabbers, while the crime-scene techs photographed the scene and began to comb the area in search of trace evidence.

"Are you all right, Dr. Madden?" Captain Black asked.

"Yes, but I know this woman." Jenny's heart clenched again as she stared at Eleanor's wide eyes. "She was a nurse on the psychiatric ward at CIRP."

He hissed. "I'm sorry. I wouldn't have asked you to come if I'd known."

She waved off his apology. "No, it's fine. I was just shocked." Determination kicked in. "But all the more reason for me to help you catch this guy before he kills again."

Black nodded and went to confer with the medical examiner while she stood back and watched them process the crime scene. She wanted to cover Eleanor and hold her, comfort her.

Detective Keegan strode over and put a hand on her back. "Captain said you were friends with our victim. I'm sorry."

"It's just so senseless," Jenny said. "She was such a nice person."

"We're almost finished here," he said in a throaty voice. "Why don't you let me drive you home? We can stop for some breakfast."

Although his invitation seemed innocent enough, something about the man disturbed her. When she glanced up, she saw Raul watching her, a fierce expression on his face. "No, thanks, Detective. Raul brought me. He'll drive me home."

"Just keep it in mind." Keegan smiled. "I have big shoulders, if you need one."

"You heard the doc," Raul cut in. "You need to work on locating the woman's family. I'll drive her and then question the hospital staff."

Keegan and Raul exchanged an odd look, all male, but Jenny didn't have time to decipher it.

Although suddenly everyone in her life seemed suspicious. Her patients. Detective Keegan. Even her brother. In fact, she didn't like her train of thought or where it was leading.

Bailey certainly seemed to be harboring a deep resentment toward women. He had an alcohol and drug problem. Was beginning to show signs of violence. Even signs of a borderline personality disorder.

He'd met Judy the night she'd died. And he could have met Eleanor at the hospital. Had he known the other victims?

CHOOSING THE NURSE from Jenny Madden's own ward was perfect. Not only would it rattle Jenny, but soon she would realize that he was coming for her.

She thought she was so smart. In control. That she knew

everything. That she could stop a man from pursuing his desires with her soothing words and stupid therapy sessions.

And now she was helping the cops. Giving them advice on how to hunt him down like an animal.

But they would never find him. He was too smart, hiding in plain sight.

It was time Jenny learned that she knew nothing. That the beast inside him couldn't be tamed. That the women got what they deserved.

And so would she.

He just had to pick the right time to show her.

Chapter Nine

"Other than the location of where he left the victim, the details of the crime scene are identical," Raul said. "CSI detected bleach on her skin, there are no traces of fluids and her body was positioned in the same manner."

Jenny shivered, and for a brief second he was tempted to comfort her again. But he had to keep his hands off. "The news reports left out those details, didn't they?"

Raul nodded. "Come on and I'll drive you to your house. Then I want to go home, clean up, drop by the hospital and question your staff."

The two of them walked to the car, and Jenny settled in while he started the engine. "Do you have time for breakfast?" he asked.

"Yes, while you were talking to the crime unit, I called my secretary and asked her to clear my schedule this morning. I wanted to leave things open for counseling the staff when they hear the news about Eleanor."

Raul headed toward Savannah where they stopped at a small café in town, and he ordered the big country breakfast while she ordered an omelet. Funny but Anita had been finicky and constantly dieting.

He had to stop comparing her to his dead wife. Anita was gone, and he wasn't looking for a replacement.

She sipped her orange juice, and looked up when she'd finished the omelet. "I thought I wouldn't have an appetite, but I eat when I'm nervous."

He smiled, and when the waitress brought the bill, she reached for it, but he grabbed it. "I woke you up in the middle of the night. This one's on me."

"Will the department reimburse you?"

Anger slammed into him. "I may not make as much money as you do, Dr. Madden, but I can buy breakfast."

She sighed and placed her hand over his. "I'm sorry, I didn't mean to insult you, Raul."

He was acting like a jerk. "I'm sorry, too. It's been a long morning."

"And the day isn't going to get any better," Jenny said softly.

"I know. Telling the victim's family is always difficult."

"I can go with you if you want," Jenny offered.

His gaze met hers. "That might help. Especially since you knew the victim."

"Could I go home and shower before we meet them?"

"Sure. Do you mind if we swing by my place first?" he asked. "It's on the way. I don't want to meet this girl's mother with the stench of her daughter's blood on my clothes."

"That's fine."

He drove to his duplex, parked and walked with Jenny up the clam-shelled drive. As they entered, he realized how cold and empty the duplex was, how he'd brought very few personal things here from South Beach. Hell, he'd left them all behind just as he left his family behind.

She looked up at him, and a deep ache clenched his gut.

He was tempted to ask Jenny to take a shower with him. He wanted to hold her again. Feel that they were both alive.

But the photo of his dead wife stared at him from the bookcase, reminding him of all he'd lost. No matter where he went he couldn't escape the memories. Or the fact that it was his fault she and his baby had been murdered.

JENNY SAW THE PAIN in Raul's eyes when he glanced at the photo on the bookshelf, and instantly knew it was a picture of his wife. Sympathy ballooned in her chest, and she started to speak, but he gestured toward the sofa. "Have a seat. I won't be long."

He disappeared into his bedroom and shut the door, cutting her out of his life, and she suddenly felt bereft. He had comforted her at the crime scene.

She wanted to do the same for him now. Wanted to knock on the door, ask him to talk. To allow her inside. To soothe the anguish on his brow and to assure him he wasn't alone anymore. That he had to go on with his life.

But she did none of those things. She couldn't push him. She had no right.

Still, she studied the face of the woman he had loved. Slender with olive skin, large amber eyes and wavy dark hair that fell to her shoulders. The sun beamed down on her where she stood on a sailboat, wearing a bikini top and sarong.

No wonder Raul had fallen for her; she was a raven beauty. Exotic and elegant, nothing like Jenny.

Sorrow for the woman and Raul tugged at her, yet irrational jealousy snaked through her, as well.

Her own father had left her when she was young, when her mother had fallen apart. Her brother was a mess himself and depended on her to take care of him. The one guy she'd dated in med school had decided her family was too screwed up to deal with. And the men she counseled in therapy were sexual deviants whose thinking was so skewed they didn't have a clue as to a normal relationship.

What would it be like to have a man like Raul love her the way he had obviously loved this woman? To commit in marriage and want her to have his child?

The door screeched open, and she glanced up and saw Raul standing in the doorway. He wore clean jeans and was buttoning up a white shirt, his bare chest peeking through the top. He'd shaved, his hair was still damp, his dark eyes skating over her as if he'd read her thoughts.

Then he zeroed in on the picture, and a muscle ticked in his jaw. "What are you doing with that?"

She almost flinched at his tone but held herself in check. "This must have been your wife. She was beautiful, Raul."

His gaze met hers, and he jerked the picture from her hands and placed it back on the shelf. "Yes, she was."

"I know that you loved her—"

"I don't want to talk about my wife," he said brusquely.

She reached for his arm, wanting to soothe his pain, to offer her friendship. "It might help if you did."

His eyes glittered dangerously. "Can you bring her back?"

"No," she said gently. "But I could help you work through your grief."

"I told you not to shrink me." He grabbed his holster from where he'd put it on the end table. "Now come on. I have a murder case to investigate. And another family to tell that their child is dead."

His words brought back a reminder of the day they faced, that her own feelings didn't matter.

That they needed to find this killer before another girl lost her life.

RAUL SILENTLY BERATED himself for his harshness, but dammit, he couldn't talk about Anita. Not to Jenny.

Especially Jenny. The first woman he'd physically wanted since his wife had died. And hell he did want her.

In the shower he'd been thinking of Jenny, not Anita. Jenny's supple curves, her long legs. That mane of beautiful golden hair. How he'd wanted her to join him.

But seeing his wife's photograph in her hand triggered his guilt to resurface, made his lustful thoughts seem wrong, as if he was betraying his wife by even thinking about another woman.

During the drive to her house, the tension between them escalated. When they arrived, she excused herself and hurried up the steps, and he heard the water kick on upstairs.

Unbidden came images of her removing her clothes, stepping naked into the shower, the water cascading over her breasts and trickling down her stomach and thighs. His body hardened, the desire to join her heating his blood.

He needed tension release. Needed to hold a warm body. Needed to feel the pleasure of pumping himself inside a woman.

Jenny. Dammit, he wanted her. He was even starting to like her. To admire her.

Which made his hunger mount.

He strode outside to the porch and gripped the rail, staring at the early-morning sun as it broke the horizon. He might want Jenny Madden, but there was no way in hell he was going to have her. His wife had died because of him.

He wouldn't take the chance on caring about anyone again.

Satisfied that he'd reined in his feelings, he stepped back inside. But upstairs he heard crying.

She'd held it together during the crime scene investigation, intended to counsel the family and others, but she was suffering herself now. He couldn't tolerate hearing her in pain.

He strode up the steps, but paused inside her bedroom. Her clothes lay on the bed, and the bathroom door stood ajar. Steam oozed through the doorway, her anguished sobs wrenching his gut, and he clutched his hands into fists, debating over what to do. Maybe she wanted to be alone.

Or maybe she needed holding. Soothing. To lean on someone else for a change.

"Jenny?"

He inched inside the doorway and found her standing naked on the floormat. She gasped when she saw him, her body trembling. Even red-faced with swollen eyes, she was more beautiful than he'd dreamed. High full breasts doused with water. Nipples rosy and extended. Curves that made his sex throb with renewed desire and sent erotic sensations to his groin.

"Raul?"

"Shh, it's okay." He removed the towel from the rack, unfolded it and wrapped it around her. Her lower lip quivered, and he pulled her in his arms. She fell against him, and he clutched her, stroking her back as she spent her emotions.

JENNY HATED TO SHOW any weakness, but she couldn't resist allowing Raul to cradle her in his arms. Like a frayed piece of cloth ripping apart at the seams, she was coming apart from the inside out. Her mother, her brother, her clients, the girls' deaths—why couldn't she save them?

She'd studied human behavior, lectured on various psychological disorders and written numerous papers, yet the very people she cared about were hurting.

Raul's arms felt so strong and comforting, his body enveloping hers as if to protect her from the pain and helplessness welling inside her. She needed that reprieve, if only for a moment.

How long had it been since she'd had a man hold her? She couldn't even remember.

And not just any man, but this tough, strong, soldier for justice who struggled each day with his own demons, who fought the violence even though he'd personally lost so much to it already.

He stroked her back and murmured calming words of comfort, and like a drowning woman, she burrowed into his chest, taking solace in the deep breaths racking him as he embraced her.

Slowly the tension dissipated in her shoulders and neck, and he lifted her chin with his thumb, then wiped her tears away with his finger. Her gaze met his, and something changed between them. Another kind of tension simmered to life, stirring sensations in her belly and a warmth that seeped through her blood. His dark eyes flickered with hunger, and his hands cupped her face, the tenderness in the gesture making her heart clench.

She wanted to kiss him. Desperately wanted a taste of the hard tough man. Wanted his hands stroking other places, assuaging the loneliness that made her ache at night when she crawled into bed alone.

As if he sensed her needs, raw passion glinted in his

eyes, and he lowered his head and kissed her. He tasted like sin and rugged male, the touch of his tongue coaxing her lips apart, sending a spark of white-hot heat streaking through her. She welcomed him inside, moaning as he thrust his tongue inside her mouth and fused their lips together. Boldly he deepened the kiss, skimming his hands down her shoulders, over her back, to her waist and hips where he pulled her closer against him. His hard length stroked her belly, pulsing with need, and she raked her hands into his hair, panting as he flicked his tongue along the sensitive skin of her neck.

She threw her head back, allowing him access, and his lips sucked at her skin, her body tingling with the need for more. To be touched everywhere. To have him inside her.

Only the towel stood between them.

That and their jobs.

But she couldn't think why that should matter, not when he trailed tongue lashes toward the curve of her breasts and his hands molded them in his palms. Her nipples tightened, and she ran her foot along his calf, hearing the rasp of his jeans as she stroked him.

She wanted his clothes off, to feel his bare chest under her hands. She reached for his shirt, felt the towel loosen at her breasts, then felt it falling to the ground. Cool air brushed her flesh, and she shivered.

He stepped back to look at her, and the smoldering look in his eyes roused her deepest desires. She'd never asked a man to make love to her, but she wanted to now.

"Raul…"

"Damn." Suddenly the hunger in his eyes changed, and regret set in. "I…we can't do this."

Hurt and humiliation stung her cheeks, and she reached for the towel.

Why had he stopped? Was he comparing her to his wife and finding her lacking?

RAUL RECOGNIZED the hurt in Jenny's expression, but he didn't know what to say.

"I'm sorry. I...overstepped my bounds."

"No," she said softly. "I wanted you—"

"Don't say that," he snapped. "It was a mistake, one we can't repeat."

Jenny grabbed her robe and dragged it on, her gaze meeting his, hurt but resigned. "I understand."

Pain laced her voice, and he hated himself for putting it there, but how could he explain? Nothing should have ever happened between them. Nothing ever could.

She brushed past him, went to her closet and began digging through it to find her clothes.

God, he was a bastard.

He stepped to the door, had to convince her that he was trying to do what was right. But she was pulling on underwear, these damn red lace panties, and he knew he had to leave or he'd take her right there in the closet.

Fists clenched, he rushed down the steps, then hurried outside. Heat suffused him, the sun glinting off the grass as he sucked in calming breaths. He'd done the right thing. Had to walk away and keep things professional. He had no right to have her or to want her so badly.

A van rolled up and parked, an older man with scruffy clothes and a limp climbing out. The man glanced up and saw him, then threw up a hand, retrieved a tool box and lumbered up the steps.

"Who are you?" Raul asked.

"Name's Ralph Martin. Dr. Madden hired me to do work around here."

"Good morning, Ralph," Jenny said behind him. "Come on in and get started. I was just leaving for work."

He lumbered in, and Jenny brushed past with her laptop and purse. She didn't look at him, simply headed toward her car.

"I could drive you," Raul offered.

"No, thanks, I'll need my car later."

Her voice was so icy that his gut clenched. Hating to leave with the strain between them, he closed the distance to her and laid his hand over hers on the door handle. "Jenny, I am sorry. I shouldn't have touched you."

She lifted her head, and emotions flickered in her eyes. "It's my fault, Raul. I know that you were married, that you loved your wife. That you had to compare me to her and find me lacking."

His mind reeled. "Is that what you think?"

She shrugged off his hand, tried to open the door but he held it shut and turned her to face him. "You think you're flawed?"

"I've been rejected before, Raul. Even my father walked away," she rasped. "I'll get over it."

So now she was filing him in the same category as her no-good deserting father. And probably the men in her groups. That pained him more than he wanted to admit.

She cleared her throat, her delicate voice vibrating with hurt, but still she jutted that little chin up. Showed courage and strength. "Now, let's get to work."

He gripped her tighter, determined to force her to listen. "You're wrong, Jenny. I didn't pull away because I was thinking of my wife or comparing her to you." His voice was hard, his own pain raw.

The confusion he felt was mirrored in her eyes, that and a vulnerability that threatened to bring him to his knees. "Then why did you stop?" she whispered.

He cleared his throat, fought the gut-churning need to kiss her again and forget his guilt and reservations.

"Raul? Please, I need to know why you don't want me."

"I do want you," he admitted tightly.

"I don't understand."

"You made me forget about my wife," he said in a gruff voice. "When I held you, kissed you, felt your body in my arms, I forgot everything but how much I wanted you." His voice cracked. "I haven't wanted a woman since that fatal night Anita died, but dammit, I wanted you, Jenny. Not her, but *you*."

"Raul—"

"But that's wrong. I have to remember or else Anita died for nothing."

Jenny lifted a hand to his cheek. The touch was so gentle his chest throbbed with the need for her tenderness. "She loved you, Raul. She would want you to go on and find happiness."

Anger and guilt stabbed at him, draining him of thought. "She wanted to be my wife, to have my baby and raise our child. So how can I be happy knowing that I'm responsible for both their deaths?"

She started to speak again, but he cut her off. He'd revealed too much already. "I can't let it go, Jenny. It's what I am now, it drives me to do my job. And that's all I have left."

His cell phone rang and he quickly connected the call.

"Cortez, it's Keegan. The victim's parents are on their way to the station."

"Dr. Madden and I will be right there." He hung up and relayed the news, and Jenny agreed to meet him at the precinct.

Knowing that if he didn't leave, he might succumb to his baser needs, he turned and stalked to his car. When he drove away, he didn't look back.

He'd have to see Jenny at the hospital, have to work with her. But there would be no more kisses. No getting naked together and sating his desires.

Only work to fuel the guilty rage eating at him.

HIS BODY HAD HARDENED as he'd sat in front of the camera and watched Jenny undress in her bedroom. She was exquisite. A helluva lot prettier than Eleanor with her dimpled legs and meek little mouth.

Jenny had curves, sweet soft curves that dipped and flared in all the right places. Skin that looked like cream and a mouth that would taste like honey. Breasts that would spill over his palms, and a throat that begged for his hands to slide around it.

He'd thought she was different, too, that she wasn't a whore. That she cared about people, cared about him.

But she was just like the others. She'd practically thrown herself at that detective, had offered herself to him without shame. Even when he'd pushed her away, Jenny had stepped forward, wanted him. Her body had revealed her secrets. Her distended nipples. Her quivering voice. Her ragged breathing.

She would quiver and pant for him when he took her. She'd cry his name and beg him to finish.

Then he'd kill her.

Chapter Ten

Raul and Jenny entered the station together, their earlier encounter still taunting him. He had to steer his mind back on track. Work was the only way to save himself and the women in town.

Captain Black met him as they entered, and he and Jenny followed him to his office.

"We're having a briefing in a few minutes," Black said. "And I've called a press conference. I don't want to create panic, but people are starting to wonder what we're doing to catch this guy. And we have to issue a warning to the women in Savannah."

A noise jarred them, and a middle-aged man and woman rushed in, looking frantic and worried. Raul exchanged a look with Black, then Jenny, and a silent understanding passed between them. Nothing they could say could alleviate the couple's anguish.

Captain Black's phone rang so he turned to answer it, and Raul greeted the couple.

"Mr. and Mrs. Stevens, I'm Detective Cortez. Please step into my office."

The wife leaned on her husband, a tissue in her hands.

Raul insisted they sit down, and Jenny followed them in and claimed a seat beside Mrs. Stevens.

"You found Eleanor, didn't you?" the husband asked.

Raul braced himself. "Yes, sir, I'm afraid we did." He paused, his tone grave. "I'm sorry to have to inform you, but she's dead."

"Oh, God, I knew it…." Mrs. Stevens broke down and began to sob, and the husband jumped up and paced to the door then leaned against it, his head bowed.

"I knew Eleanor, she was a wonderful nurse." Jenny gathered the sobbing woman into her arms and held her, relaying the staff's affection and respect for her daughter.

Mr. Stevens turned to him, tears glittering in his eyes, but his jaw was set as if determined to be a Rock of Gibraltar for his wife. "What happened?"

This part was even more difficult. Jenny gave him a sympathetic look, and he began. "I'm sorry, but she was strangled, Mr. Stevens."

Anger flamed the father's face. "You're talking about that serial killer, aren't you? That damn psycho got my daughter." Stevens grabbed Raul by the collar. "Why haven't you found him before now? What in the hell are you cops doing?" His voice cracked, all calmness disintegrating. "If you had him off the streets, my girl would be alive."

Raul pried Stevens's hands loose, but tempered his tone. "I understand your anger, sir, but trust me when I say we're doing everything possible to find this man."

"It's not enough," Stevens barked.

"Can we see our baby?" Mrs. Stevens rasped.

"I'll talk to the M.E.," Raul said. "But I need to ask you some questions first."

"Why?" Mr. Stevens snapped. "You should be out hunting down this killer—"

"Mr. Stevens," Jenny interrupted. "It's important that we know everything about Eleanor's friends and schedule. She may have been abducted by someone she knew, someone she was dating or a recent acquaintance."

Mrs. Stevens sniffed, then pleaded with her husband to sit back down. "We'll help you any way we can."

Raul nodded. This woman was every bit as strong as her husband. It was a good thing, too, because he understood firsthand how grief and anger could destroy a person.

Jenny's compassion sent a sliver of warmth through him, erasing the chill in his body, a chill he'd had ever since Anita's death.

Yet Jenny had made him feel alive again, had made him want a relationship. And that scared him more than anything. He wanted to stay dead.

Because as long as he was dead inside, he couldn't feel that kind of pain again.

SYMPATHY AND FRUSTRATION knotted Jenny's shoulders as she watched Raul question the couple. Unfortunately their daughter had moved into her own apartment, hadn't mentioned dating anyone or received any threats.

"I'm going to search Eleanor's apartment, and confiscate her computer," Raul told them. "Maybe something will turn up there to give us a lead."

"Please find him," Mrs. Stevens implored.

"I promise I won't give up until we do," Raul assured her.

Mr. Stevens gave him a wary look, but had calmed and thanked Raul, then the couple left, huddled together in their grief.

Captain Black called a debriefing, so Raul, Keegan and the other local officers gathered, Jenny included.

"This is what we have so far," Raul said. "Four victims, all women. We found a wood sliver beneath one girl's nail. Trace said it was oak, paint a builder's grade. Not much to go on, but it might help."

"No fingerprints," Keegan added. "And that partial boot-print might help if we had someone to match it to. Forensics estimated it to be from a male, size thirteen, meaning our guy is probably tall, a big man." He hesitated. "Still nothing on the panties."

Black cleared his throat. "About the sex, forensics found traces of Rohypnol in Eleanor Stevens's body just like Judy Benson's."

"How about that credit card? Anything more?" Raul asked.

"Card is in the name of Bobby Machete, address originated in Atlanta. Still haven't located the man."

Jenny clutched the chair edge. "Bobby Machete?"

Keegan nodded.

"Why? Do you recognize the name, Jenny?" Raul asked.

Perspiration trickled down her neck. "Yes," she said. "He was a patient of mine in Atlanta, but he died a month before I left."

The room grew silent, tension thrumming as minds swirled.

"What caused his death?" Raul asked.

"A car accident, I think," Jenny replied.

"Could be another Bobby Machete?" Keegan interjected.

Captain Black rapped his knuckles on the table. "Find out. Could be a case of stolen identity and this is our perp."

Keegan piped up. "His mail has been forwarded to a PO

box here in Savannah. Maybe they have security cameras, and we can get a picture."

Hushed murmurs filled the room, a tinge of excited hope brightening the bleak mood.

"Let's get to it, people," Black said. "And keep me in the loop."

They scattered, although Black asked Raul to handle the press conference and Jenny followed him outside, her head pinging with thoughts of her Atlanta patients and Bobby Machete.

Several reporters along with locals had gathered on the steps to the precinct, the tension high between the cops and the press who wanted someone to blame for the fact that the killer hadn't been caught.

"We want to caution women to be alert, to travel in pairs, to watch your drinks in a bar or social situation, to alert the police if you see anything suspicious, if a stranger approaches you that seems odd," Raul said. "If you know anything about these women that might help us or about the killer, please notify the police."

"We need more details," a reporter yelled. "Is he raping the women before he kills them?"

"I'm not at liberty to divulge any details," Raul said. "We don't want to tip our hand in case we get a viable suspect."

"Do you have any suspects?" another reporter shouted.

"No one that we can name at this time." Raul cut them off and strode back inside, fending off more reporters and questions.

Jenny wove through the throng to her car and drove to work. She had to talk to the staff at CIRP, offer grief counseling to those who knew Eleanor and put her own feelings aside. Nothing mattered except catching this guy.

On the way to the hospital, though, she called Bailey. His comment about her mother disturbed her, and she wanted an explanation for why he'd debase her mother.

"What in the hell do you want this early?" His voice sounded groggy with sleep. Either that or he was hung over.

"Why did you call Mom a tramp?"

"Because she was," Bailey snapped. "She cheated on Dad, that's why he left."

"What?" Jenny's heart stopped. "What makes you say that, Bailey?"

"You're so naive, Jenny. I saw her myself," he growled. "Humping and grinding right there in our own house with another man." He hesitated. "And more than once."

No… "Bailey, are you sure?"

"Hell, yeah, I'm sure. I'll never forget it."

His voice broke, and she realized that Bailey had been shattered by that sight. That it had affected him ever since.

"It was sickening, Jen," he cried. "The first time I saw them, I threw up all night."

Emotions swirled in Jenny's chest. "Good heavens, Bailey, you should have told me. Who was the man?"

"I don't know," he said, his voice shrill. "It was dark and I was just a kid. I didn't go in, didn't want to see his face." He paused, gulping a breath. "Maybe you should ask Mom. But that's why Dad walked out."

He should have stayed for us.

Jenny gripped the steering wheel. "Please come and see me, and let's talk."

"Talking won't do any good," Bailey said.

He hung up, and worry nagged at Jenny. But she'd arrived at the hospital and work awaited. First she had to break the news of Eleanor's death to the staff.

Then she'd talk to Dr. Solaris and relay what Bailey had revealed. Maybe in his session, he could uncover what had really happened with her mother. If her affair had led to her divorce, if guilt had led to her psychotic break or if there was more to the story.

RAUL AND KEEGAN DROVE to Eleanor Stevens's apartment and met the superintendent of the building, but he claimed he knew nothing about Eleanor except that she seemed like a nice girl.

Inside they searched her desk and found a calendar with a note for a doctor's appointment, but no mention of personal dates or relationships. Raul's preliminary check of her computer showed e-mail to a couple of female friends, and another to a guy inquiring about the nursing program but he lived in Alabama.

He checked further and found a MySpace account.

"Keegan, did any of the other girls have MySpace accounts?"

"Tech was looking into it."

If so, it might be a connection. He checked Eleanor's list of friends but none of the girls were on it, unless they had used fake names. "Take Eleanor's computer to tech and have them cross-check all her mail and MySpace friends with names from the other girls' computers."

"That'll take time."

"If it leads us to the killer, it's worth it. Oh, and tell them to look for anything from Bobby Machete."

Keegan nodded.

"Also, find out where Jamal Rakely was last night. I'm going to stop by Clyde Anson's and question him, then talk to the hospital staff. Maybe someone there knows who Eleanor might have been seeing."

Keegan confiscated the computer and carried it to the squad car. Raul headed to Anson's house to meet him face-to-face. He wanted to see his reaction to the girls' deaths, let him know that, if he was guilty, Raul was onto him.

Heat blazed through the car as he drove to Anson's, parked and knocked on Anson's door. At first, no response, so he pounded again and rang the doorbell. Finally the door squeaked open, and a muscular body builder type with bleary eyes frowned at him.

"Detective Cortez, SPD." Raul flashed his badge. "Clyde Anson?"

"Yeah." He scrubbed a hand over his stubble-covered chin. "What do you want?"

Raul glanced at the street, at cars passing by, at a kid on a bike watching them. "Can I come in?"

Anson mumbled a profanity, but opened the door and gave him access. Raul immediately zeroed in on the newspapers spread on the table. Anson had cut out the articles on the Savannah Strangler and taped them on his refrigerator.

"I see you're interested in the serial killer stalking women in Savannah."

Anson gave a lopsided smile, then walked to the counter and put on a pot of coffee. "Just curious like everyone else in town, I guess."

The coffee began to drip through the filter in a steady rhythm, the only sound in the dingy place except for the tension thrumming through the air.

"Are you sure it's just curiosity?" Raul's voice hardened. "I know about your history of violence."

Anson's laser-sharp look held a touch of evil and confirmed what Raul already knew—this man was dangerous.

But he was going to play the game.

"I paid my dues," Anson said, removing a mug from the cabinet. "Rehabilitating myself, you know. Got me a pretty little doc to hold my hand and a bunch of pills to control my urges."

Fury raced through Raul's veins. "Maybe you're putting on an act?"

Anson feigned an innocent look. "Don't know what you're talking about. Me, I get to lie on Doc's couch and look up at her big eyes. And those legs and body. Don't get much better than that."

Raul knotted his hands into fists. "Where were you last night?"

"Working at the Universal Joint," Anson said smoothly. "You can check it out with the manager."

He removed the photos of the victims and spread them on the table. "You know any of these girls?"

Anson gave them a brief glance. "No. Not my type."

As if Jenny was. "I'm watching you, Anson. Remember that." He snatched up the photos. "And make sure you keep your hands off that doc, or you'll end up back in the can."

Anson's gaze narrowed, and Raul realized he'd tipped his hand. From the articles, Anson obviously knew Raul was working with her. But now he knew that Raul had a personal interest, too.

He'd warn Jenny to watch out for the man.

And if Anson laid a finger on her, Raul would throw him back in jail and make sure he never got out.

JENNY SPENT most of the morning counseling staff members who were distraught over the news of Eleanor's death. She also provided a buffer when Raul arrived and questioned them.

Theresa, an RN who had befriended Eleanor, dabbed at her tears. "She was so sweet. I talked to her yesterday before she finished her shift. She had a date for coffee."

"Was her date someone she knew already?"

"No, it was a first date."

"How did they meet?"

She twisted her mouth sideways. "On the Internet. She was so shy that it was easier for her to talk online. She joined one of those matchmaking services. She really wanted to find Mr. Right, settle down and have a family."

"Didn't she realize that's not safe, that there're all kinds of perverts and scam artists on the Internet?" Raul asked.

"That's the reason she was only meeting him for coffee." Theresa's tone turned defensive. "A public place, no alcohol. She didn't give him her home number or address, either."

Jenny sighed. Eleanor was trying to be smart, thought she was taking precautions. But someone could have slipped a drug in her coffee just as they could have in a mixed drink or glass of wine.

"Our tech team is checking out her computer. Maybe that will lead to something concrete," he told the young woman.

She nodded, but grief had set in along with shock. "I should have gone with her, sat at another table, made sure she was safe."

Jenny urged Theresa to sit down. "It's not your fault, Theresa, and we're not here to cast blame. We just want to find the man who did this and get him off the streets."

Theresa sniffled and nodded, although she still looked tormented by guilt.

Dr. Solaris appeared, his glasses perched on the end of his nose. "Dr. Madden, I'd like to speak with you when you have a moment. It's important."

"I'll be right there." She patted Theresa on the back. "Will you be okay?"

"Yes, thank you for being here, Jenny."

"Just call me if you need to talk. Anytime day or night."

She excused herself and headed toward Dr. Solaris's office, but Raul cornered her. "Jenny, this guy might be one of your patients. I spoke with Clyde Anson this morning. He has cutouts of all the articles on the case, and he's dangerous. If you won't talk to me about him, I'm going to request a warrant for your files."

Resignation set in. "Do what you have to do, Raul. And so will I."

A silent understanding passed between them. She'd made the same comment before. They both wanted this guy bad. But they had to follow protocol. Jenny's patients had to be assured that she hadn't offered them up or they might come after her.

"I have to see Dr. Solaris now," Jenny said.

He stared at her for a heartbeat, then nodded.

Wariness registered in his eyes as she claimed a chair in Dr. Solaris's office facing his desk. "What's wrong, Doctor? Is my mother worse? Did she have another episode?"

"Not exactly." He tapped a pen on the desk as if toying with how much to reveal. "I don't like to discuss my patients with anyone, you know that."

"Yes. But—"

"But I need to know if your mother had any relationships with men other than your father."

Jenny's heart raced. "As a matter of fact, earlier today Bailey had an outburst, and told me that when he was small, he saw Mom in bed with another man."

Dr. Solaris's lips thinned. "I see."

"What?" She gripped the chair edge with clammy palms. "Why are you asking me this?"

He released a pent-up breath and she sensed bad news.

"I don't have definitive proof, but I think I may have discovered the root of your mother's breakdown."

Jenny's breath stalled in her chest. Getting to the crux of the problem meant hope. "Go on."

He nodded solemnly. "Actually there are two problems. I told you I thought your mother was overmedicated."

"Yes."

"I firmly believe that now. But I also have reason to believe that she suffered a trauma that triggered her spiral into depression and psychosis."

"What kind of trauma?" Jenny asked.

"You aren't going to like this, Jenny." He stood, circled the desk then claimed the chair beside her.

"I've lived without a mother all these years, Dr. Solaris. I can handle whatever news you have. I just want her to get better."

"Very well." His stern brows pulled together into a frown. "According to preliminary tests and interviews with your mother, I believe she was raped."

Jenny gasped. "What? When?"

"It started years ago. Before your brother was born."

"What do you mean it started?"

He crossed one leg over the other, the tension building until she could hardly stand it.

"Please just tell me."

He cleared his throat, folded his hands. "There are signs indicating that your mother has been sexually abused for years."

Waves of shock rolled through Jenny. She twisted her hands, her breathing labored. "Physical signs?"

"Yes. And from your mother's comments, as well."

Jenny gulped. "My God, who did it?" Realization slowly dawned, and she stared at him, her heart pounding. "You think someone in the treatment center raped her? That they kept her medicated so she couldn't reveal the abuse?"

"Not just someone," he said with conviction. "Her former doctor. Dr. Zovall."

Jenny's mind reeled, a devastating sense of betrayal knifing through her. It couldn't be. Dr. Zovall had been a family friend to her and Bailey. A mentor to her. He'd encouraged her to attend medical school, to become a therapist. And Bailey.

God. Poor Bailey.

He thought he had seen their mother having an affair. What if he'd really witnessed their mother's rape?

RUPERT ZOVALL KNEW his time was almost up. By now, the doctors at CIRP might have discovered that he'd overmedicated Marilyn.

But hopefully they didn't know the rest.

Damn Jenny for moving her mother. Damn her to hell and back.

He'd worked all his life to earn his reputation. And he'd

covered his tracks for years now. He wouldn't let that little bitch destroy his life.

He should have taken care of her like he had her mother years ago. Should have had her as his own.

Funny how she'd never turned him on, though. Too haughty and cold. An ice queen with a smart mouth. He'd only tolerated her so he could stay close to her mother.

And to Bailey.

He'd take care of Jenny now. He had to or his future was ruined.

Then he'd finish off Marilyn, too. Tonight he'd slip into her room. One dose and she'd be back to her vegetative state. Then he'd give her another cocktail, a specialty of his own. Then she wouldn't talk.

She'd carry his secrets with her to her grave.

Chapter Eleven

Questions bombarded Jenny. Was it true? Had Dr. Zovall abused her mother all these years? Was that the reason he'd protested her decision to move her mother to CIRP? The reason he'd stalled in sending records to Dr. Solaris?

The reason he'd monitored her and Bailey's visits over the years?

She had to talk to Bailey, find out exactly what he'd seen. If he had witnessed his mother's rape, no wonder he was confused, had had problems all these years. He had suffered a trauma, too, and at a young age.

"If this is true, why didn't I see what was going on?" Jenny asked. "All those years and I had no clue…"

"You were a kid yourself when it started," Dr. Solaris said. "As you grew older, your mother wasn't coherent enough to discuss what happened. Either she repressed the memories or she was too delusional to distinguish reality from fantasy."

"Because she was so drugged," Jenny cried. "Dr. Zovall kept her that way so he could continue abusing her." Tears trickled down her cheeks as bitterness mushroomed inside her. "Mom must have suffered so much, felt so alone."

"Have you spoken with Dr. Zovall lately?" Dr. Solaris asked.

Jenny shook her head. "No." Which was odd in itself. He should have called to check on her mother. "Have you been in contact with him?"

"No, I've tried to contact him several times, but he hasn't responded to my calls or e-mails. And his secretary said he had to go away for a few days. That he left suddenly. But she left him a message saying that he needed to contact me immediately."

Panic seized Jenny. "What if he's on his way here now or already in Savannah? What if he comes after my mother?"

Concern darkened the doctor's eyes. "We have security, and I'll make sure her room is watched," Dr. Solaris said. "But I'd like the police to bring him in for questioning."

Anger rallied, filling her with determination. "Detective Cortez is here talking to the staff about Eleanor. I'll ask him." She clutched the doctor's hands. "Please take care of my mother, be sure to watch her room. After I speak with the detective, I have to see Bailey."

Dr. Solaris stood. "All right, and, Jenny, I know this is bad, but remember that unearthing the problem is the first step in solving it. I believe there's a chance that with time your mother can recover."

Hope fluttered in Jenny's heart for the first time in years. She really might get her mother back.

But what about Bailey? How would he feel when he realized his mother hadn't willingly slept with another man, that she'd been forced? That no one in the family had a clue as to what was going on?

That no one had saved her from the man who was supposed to be helping her?

ALARM STOLE THROUGH RAUL as he spotted Jenny leaving the doctor's office. Her eyes were red, her face pale and she was trembling. Had something happened to her mother?

In two quick strides, he crossed the hall to her. She let out a small shriek when he grabbed her arm.

"Jenny, what's wrong?"

For a tense second she looked dazed, as if in pain or shock. Then she blinked and seemed to realize that he'd asked her a question.

"I was coming to find you," she said.

He pulled her into a corner away from nurses and orderlies passing. "What happened? You look upset."

She shivered against him. "I have to talk to my brother. But I need a favor."

"Of course, but first tell me what in the hell is wrong."

"Can you put an APB out on Dr. Rupert Zovall?"

The fact that she'd ignored his question raised his suspicion.

"Who is he, Jenny? Does he have something to do with the Strangler?"

"No, no. My mother," she whispered hoarsely. "He was her doctor back in Atlanta."

Confusion made him narrow his eyes. "For God's sake, Jenny, I'm not going to advertise your mother's illness, but I have to have a reason to issue an arrest warrant for someone." He wanted to shake her, convince her to talk. "Trust me. And I'll do whatever I can."

She glanced around as if to make certain no one was listening. Then she lowered her voice. "Dr. Solaris thinks Dr. Zovall overmedicated my mother. He suspects the doctor raped her and kept her drugged so he could continue abusing her all these years."

Bile rose in Raul's throat. Now he understood the pain and grief in her eyes. She'd trusted this doctor and he'd betrayed her. Even worse, he'd betrayed his oath to his patients and taken advantage of his position for his own sick twisted needs.

He wanted to pull her in his arms, hold her, comfort her, assure her everything would work out. But the best thing he could do was to find this doctor and make him pay. He'd stolen a woman's life, and a mother from her own child.

He brushed at the tears she didn't even realize she'd let fall. "I'll find him, Jenny, I promise. And we'll put him away."

Her fine-boned hand clutched at his arm. "Thank you, Raul. Now I have to talk to Bailey and explain to him what's going on."

Remembering her brother's volatile behavior, he held her back. "Let me go with you."

"No." She squeezed his hand. "Thank you for offering, Raul. But this is something I have to do alone. It's not going to be easy for Bailey to hear, but he has to know the truth."

He hesitated, hated for her to face her brother alone. But he had to respect her privacy. After all, he had no claims on her, was not a part of her family. Still he was worried…
"All right. But call me if you need me."

She nodded, then ran down the hall. His heart clenched. He wanted to help her, but somehow nothing he could do seemed enough.

JENNY INSTRUCTED RENEE to cancel her appointments for the remainder of the day, then dialed Bailey's number as she hurried to the elevator. By the time she reached her car, he finally answered.

"Two calls in one day from the great doctor in the family," he said sarcastically. "To what do I owe this honor?"

He slurred his last words, and she gritted her teeth, hesitating over whether she should wait, but she decided now was as good a time as any. Besides, she had to know if Dr. Solaris was right, if Bailey's young mind had misunderstood what had transpired in their house. "I need to see you, Bailey."

"Thought you didn't want anything to do with your baby brother."

She had to reach him somehow. "Just tell me where you are and I'll come to you. It's really important or I wouldn't ask."

"Yeah, so was my asking you for a cover, and you turned me down."

She clutched the phone with a white-knuckled grip. "I'll bring money, Bailey. Just meet me or tell me where you are dammit."

He hesitated, and for a moment she thought he intended to hang up. But then desperation laced his voice, "You'll bring me some cash?"

"Yes," she said, though her jaw ached from biting back a lecture.

"All right, then. I'm holed up at that rathole of a motel outside of town where I stayed last time."

She should have known. "I'll be there as soon as I run by an ATM."

She hung up and started the car, then spun out of the parking lot. The bank first, where she withdrew five hundred dollars, then maneuvered the car through traffic to the motel. Rain clouds hovered above, obliterating any remaining sun, the gray skies threatening.

She inhaled several deep breaths in an attempt to calm her nerves, but anger and contempt knotted her insides. Nevertheless she was the professional here, the big sister. She had to prepare herself to deal with Bailey if he fell apart.

At home later she could have her own meltdown.

Her tires squealed as she rolled into the parking lot and slammed on the brakes. With a heavy heart, she climbed out, locked her door, then jogged to the motel door. She knocked twice, heard footsteps and muttering, then Bailey opened the door. He looked terrible, unshaven, wore a T-shirt with holes in it and a pair of ragged jeans. He smelled of sweat and booze.

Realizing he was high, she started to back away. He might handle the conversation better if he was straight, but when would that be?

One eyebrow lifted as he leaned against the door. "You got the cash?"

She shoved the envelope in his hand. "Five hundred, and don't spend it on alcohol or drugs. Clean yourself up, Bailey, and get a job."

He swung out his arm in anger. "If you came here to bitch at me again, then get the hell out."

She sighed, pushed her way inside, disgusted at the beer cans and empty pizza boxes stacked on the scarred dresser. "I didn't come to gripe at you, Bailey. I told you this is really important. We have to talk."

"That's all you do. You think talking fixes everything," he shouted, "but it didn't work with Mom and it sure as hell won't work with me."

"Just shut up and listen, Bailey."

Her harsh tone took him off guard, and he staggered back and dropped into the chair.

Her concession had been the money; she refused to cut him any slack. She needed answers and he might hold the key to the truth. "This is serious. It's about Mom."

For a moment pain flickered in his eyes and he looked like a lost little boy, but belligerence quickly replaced the innocent look. "What she'd do? Die?"

Jenny gasped. "Is that what you want, Bailey? Do you hate her that much?"

He scrubbed his hands over his face, then shook his head, the glazed pain back in his eyes. "So what happened?"

"I just came from talking to Dr. Solaris. He thinks he's uncovered the trigger for Mom's illness."

His gaze met hers, questioning, waiting, afraid. She wanted to shield him from the pain, but only the truth could enable them to start the healing process.

"Bailey," she said gently. "Dr. Solaris believes that Mom has been abused for years. That Dr. Zovall overmedicated her, that he raped her years ago before you were even born, and kept her drugged to keep her quiet."

His mouth gaped open, shock turning his face a sickly green.

"Could Dr. Zovall have been the man you saw with Mom? The one you thought she was having an affair with?"

"She was cheating on him. I saw her, dammit, I told Dad!"

She gave him a second to assimilate what she'd said, knew he was probably retracing memories of the past. "Are you sure? You were only what, four? Maybe you misunderstood what was going on."

Bailey suddenly vaulted up, paced to the window,

leaned against the edge, heaving for air. "No…yes. I mean, I don't know. I was little…I didn't want to look, to see what was going on." A cry ripped from deep inside him. "I just knew it was wrong. Ugly."

Jenny's heart bled. She walked over and pressed a hand to his shoulder, rubbing circles around his back to relieve his tension. "You were just a child, Bailey. It must have been horrible finding the two of them in bed. And Mom… was she upset? Was he holding her down?"

"I heard her crying," he said quietly, "heard her more than once. But I didn't understand."

He spun around, hurt and other emotions that frightened her sparkling in his eyes. "Are you sure it was rape, Jenny? This doc could be wrong."

"Dr. Solaris wouldn't have told me if he didn't have good reason to suspect it's true."

"You trusted Dr. Zovall, too."

His barb cut deep. "Yes," she admitted in a gravelly voice. "And I'll never forgive myself for that. But I was young, too, Bailey, when this all happened. Dr. Solaris has no reason to lie to me, not like Dr. Zovall did if he was covering up a crime."

His face twisted with rage, but she continued. "I've asked Raul…Detective Cortez to bring him in for questioning."

As if the horror of the situation dawned on him, Bailey began to shake. Huge wails of anger and pain echoed from his throat. "It's my fault, isn't it? I saw Mom being attacked and I let it happen."

"No," Jenny said softly. "No, Bailey, you couldn't have known what was going on."

"But you think it's my fault, that I should have spoken up," he screeched. "And I told Dad and he saw them, and then he left. So it's my fault he ran out on us, too…" His voice cracked. "Why didn't he figure it out?"

Emotions clogged her throat, but Jenny refrained from replying. Maybe her father had known and he'd left anyway. Maybe he'd learned about the initial rape, that Bailey might not be his son, and he couldn't deal with it.

"I'm not saying that at all," she replied. "Children can't be held responsible for adult problems. Neither one of us were old enough to understand."

Bailey pounded his fist on the glass with such force a pane shattered. Jenny reached out to see if he was cut, but he shoved her so hard she fell backward, and her head hit the side table. Pain shot through her temple and the room spun.

"You said he raped her before I was born." Pure rage glittered in his glazed eyes and Bailey went ballistic, swinging his bloody fist, kicking the table and screaming obscenities.

"Bailey, stop it. Please calm down."

His chest heaved up and down. "So what's the bottom line? That Mom is ill because of me and this doctor, that I'm what—his bastard son?"

Jenny struggled to pull herself up, a small streak of blood trickling down her forehead. But Bailey sprang at her again, grabbed her arms and began to shake her.

"Stop it, Bailey, let me go," she cried. "Let's talk."

He shook her again, knocking the breath from her chest, and she clawed at his arms, pleading with him to let her go.

Suddenly a knock sounded on the door. "What's going on in there?" a man shouted from the other side.

She shoved at Bailey, and the knock came again.

"Open the door or I'm calling the cops!" the man yelled.

The door swung open, and Bailey hesitated like a small

animal trapped by a predator. But he released her abruptly, ran outside, jumped in his old car and raced off.

The elderly man who must have been the manager of the motel, hobbled over. "Are you okay, miss? You want me to call the cops?"

Jenny straightened her clothing, wiping at her forehead. "No, please don't call anyone. I'm all right."

The age lines around his mouth deepened with his scowl. "Are you sure? You can't let him get away with that, miss. It's not right."

"He's my brother," Jenny said. "And he just had some shocking news. I…I'll see that he receives help."

She grabbed her purse, her head and heart aching as she rushed to her car. Silent tears slid down her cheeks as she drove through Savannah. A family strolling along together, mothers pushing baby strollers, couples walking dogs—she searched her memory to find a semblance of her family doing the same. But all she remembered was the arguments and dissension, her father's back as he walked out the door, her mother shutting down more and more each day.

Thankfully Ralph had gone when she arrived home, but she smelled the fresh paint and realized he'd painted the kitchen and dining room in one day. Ironic how nice her house was progressing when her life was completely disintegrating in front of her eyes.

She ran up the steps, threw off her clothes, climbed in the shower and gave her emotions full rein. The last time she'd done that Raul had been here, and he'd held her while she cried.

There was no one here tonight. She was alone as she always had been.

But her brother and mother were hurting the most. And there were still women dying in the town.

She had done nothing to help any of them. Maybe Raul was right. What good was she to anyone if she couldn't help her own family? If she'd been so blind that she hadn't seen what was going on with the ones she loved most?

And what would Bailey do now?

Was he Dr. Zovall's son?

Her analytical skills kicked in. Dr. Zovall was a rapist… but too old to be the Strangler.

Yet Bailey fit the profile. She'd seen the hatred in his eyes tonight. He detested women, felt betrayed. He'd suffered a trauma at a young age.

He was on the edge. Would he take his rage out on someone else?

She'd told Raul she'd call the police if Bailey touched her again. And tonight he had wanted to hurt her. But could she turn her brother in to the police? If she did and he was innocent, he would never forgive her and she'd lose any chance they had to glue their shattered family back together.

But if she didn't, and he hurt someone, the next girl's death would be on her head.

RAUL CONTACTED HIS CAPTAIN about a warrant for Jenny's files and an APB for Zovall, finished questioning the staff, then returned to the station and called the tech team where he learned that all four of the vics had MySpace accounts.

Eleanor had befriended three guys in cyberspace and agreed to meet them at different times for coffee. The team was running a trace to find out real names and addresses and investigate common friends.

Keegan loped in, looking smug. "It looks like we might

be able to trace the panties the killer uses," he said. "Bought them online, but they were shipped to a post office box, the one that belonged to Machete."

"Good work," Raul said. Hopefully with the MySpace accounts they might be able to track this guy down and catch him. Especially if they linked him to Bobby Machete.

He just hoped they could arrest the guy before another girl died.

Worried about Jenny, he punched her number while Keegan called forensics to see if they'd found anything at the last crime scene. She didn't answer her cell so he phoned her landline, but no answer there, either. He left a message in both places for her to call him, then hung up, still antsy. He didn't like her brother one damn bit, and wondered how he'd reacted to the news about their mother.

Still, he had work to do on the case, so he carried Eleanor's picture with him to show to the local coffee houses in town.

Two hours later he was beat. One waitress at a coffee shop near the hospital recognized Eleanor but didn't remember seeing her with a man.

Worried, he headed toward home, but tried Jenny again. Finally she answered.

"It's Raul. How did things go with Bailey?"

"Not good," she admitted quietly. So quietly that alarm shot through him.

"I'm coming over."

"No," she said quickly. "Really, Raul, I'm tired, it was a trying day."

"You don't sound tired, you sound upset. What happened?"

"Naturally Bailey was upset. But we'll work through it."

He clutched the phone with a white-knuckled grip. "Did he hurt you, Jenny?"

A heartbeat of silence followed where he found himself holding his breath. "No, I'm just really exhausted. Don't worry about me, Raul. I've been taking care of myself a long time. I'll be fine."

She said good-night and hung up, leaving Raul feeling oddly helpless and alone. The sadness in her tone tugged at him, and he almost spun the car around toward her house, but remembered his vow not to touch her again.

It was better to leave things this way. If he saw her tonight, he'd forget that vow.

He'd make love to her, and then he'd want more.

And caring only led to pain, pain he didn't need or want to feel again....

IT TOOK EVERY OUNCE of restraint Jenny possessed not to beg Raul to come over. She wanted his arms around her holding her all night, whispering that he cared. Letting her know that all men weren't bad. That he'd make everything all right.

That she mattered to him and that for once someone would take care of her.

But nothing was all right. Women were in danger from a sexual deviant who very well might be one of the men in her care. One she obviously hadn't healed.

Her brother was falling apart. Blaming himself for something that happened years ago, something that wasn't his fault. Something that had traumatized him and affected him his entire life.

And her mother...her poor mother...would have to come to terms with the truth and the years that she'd lost. That is, if they could save her from her own traumatized mind.

And her father—where did he fit in this? Had he known the truth, that her mother was raped? Did he think she'd had an affair? Did he know that Bailey might not be his son? Was that the reason he'd left?

Hugging her arms around herself, she battled the emotions pummeling her. She felt so bereft and alone. She wanted Raul….

But he was still in love with his wife. People who'd lost loved ones to violence or early death often placed them on pedestals. She could never live up to the perfect image he had of his wife.

Not when she was a failure at everything she'd tried to do in her life.

Aching inside, she steeped a cup of hot tea and sipped it, then wearily settled into bed. All she wanted to do was sleep. Sleep and shut out the voices in her head. The cries of the victims who had died. The pleas of the patients who needed her.

The sound of her mother's silent scream for help…

She closed her eyes, but nightmares haunted her. The dead girls' wide eyes stared at her asking why they'd died. Bailey appeared there, too, the rage in his voice taunting her that the girls had gotten what they deserved.

Next floated a sea of faces—Jamal Rakely, Clyde Anson, Carl, the man in the group who had a fetish for satin and silk, Dr. Zovall laughing at her stupidity as he pretended to care for her mother.

A squeak of the floor jarred her awake, and she opened her eyes, her heart pounding. Another squeak, then a subtle breath rasping in the darkness.

She wasn't alone.

Fear immobilizing her, her chest heaved and she quickly

scanned the room. The curtain fluttered, a storm raging outside. A shadow moved toward her, hands outstretched.

She screamed and tried to reach for the phone, but he knocked it off the nightstand and it clattered to the floor. She threw up her hands to fight, but he slapped her so hard she saw black, then he pressed his knee into her stomach, and grasped her neck.

His heavy weight held her prisoner as he tightened his grip, choking the air from her lungs. Her body bucked, the blackness threatening to consume her.

Panic set in. She was going to die and she'd never see Raul again.

Chapter Twelve

Jenny couldn't give up. She struggled against her attacker, swinging her hand sideways for something to defend herself, but she grasped at dead air.

The man wrapped something silky around her throat and was using it to choke her. A tie? Silk scarf? Panties?

God, was it the Strangler?

He pulled tighter, and she gasped for air, grappling for a weapon, and finally her fingers closed around the bedside clock. She swung it up and slammed it into the side of his head. The blow jarred him just enough to loosen his hold, and she raised her knee and thrust it against his groin. He howled, and punched her across the face, and stars shot before her eyes. The world swirled, but she used both feet to kick him, this time funneling all her strength into the jab until she knocked him backward and off her. His body bounced against the wall.

Taking advantage of the moment, she rolled off the bed and raced toward the door. He lunged after her, but she sidestepped him, then fled through the door. Without power or moonlight, the house was so dark, she couldn't see two feet in front of her, and outside thunder ripped, exploding in the sky. Rain slashed the roof, but footsteps sounded behind her, and she heard breathing rasping closer.

Feeling her way down the stairs, she hit the bottom one and clawed her way to the umbrella stand. Heart pounding, she grabbed the umbrella, then swung it at the man's legs as he descended the last step. She must have hit him below the knees because he tripped and cursed, a muted sound beneath the roar of the wind as his knees connected with the floor.

She didn't wait for him to recover, but raced to her office, slammed the door and locked it, then grabbed the phone and dialed 911.

"This is Dr. Jenny Madden. Someone's in my house. He tried to kill me."

He shook the door and jerked at the doorknob then tried to kick his way in.

"Your location, ma'am?"

Her pulse racing, she blurted out her address. "Please hurry!"

More kicking at the door. Wood splintered.

"We'll have someone there ASAP. Is he armed, ma'am?"

"I don't know. Hurry! He's trying to kick down the door." She slammed down the phone and dragged the chair over in front of it.

Outside, something slashed the window pane, and she screamed, pivoting to see if he'd come around to break through the window. It looked like claws scratching at the glass—hands? A tree limb?

Panic tightened her lungs, and she shrieked as thunder boomed again. She backed into the corner, her gaze jumping from the window to the door, waiting, wondering which one he would break through.

Her mind swirled with thoughts of a weapon. In the office there was nothing but her computer. She'd boxed up things so Ralph could paint.

Hoping he'd left his toolbox inside when he'd repaired the molding, she felt along the floor edge. Her hand touched the cold metal, and she fumbled with the latch, then felt around until her hand closed around the hammer. She gripped it in her hand and braced herself. If the man burst in, she'd have to fight him with it.

RAUL'S PHONE JANGLED as he left the last coffee shop and checked the number. His captain. He connected the call. "Cortez."

"Raul, a 911 call just came in from Dr. Madden's house. I thought you'd want to know."

Raul's heart raced. "I'll be there in five." He hung up, spun around and hit the accelerator. The raging storm mimicked his pounding pulse as he flipped on his siren, bypassed slower traffic and honked for cars to move out of the way. He dashed through a red light, tires skidding as he careened onto Jenny's street.

His chest tightened as he spotted her house. All the lights were out, yet lights still burned at the neighbors' two doors down. Someone must have intentionally tampered with her power. Dammit.

Had her brother gotten violent? Had that doctor resurfaced?

Or could the Strangler have come after Jenny?

Fear knifed through his chest as he cut the siren and his headlights. He slammed on the breaks and parked at the curb three houses away, wanting to catch whoever it was, instead of alerting him of his arrival. From his peripheral vision, he saw a shadow lurking around the corner of the house and up the porch steps.

He threw open the car door and hit the ground running, then crouched down and eased along the red tips up the drive. Scanning the property as he moved, he braced himself to fire, staying partially hidden by the bushes.

"Stop or I'll shoot." He raised his gun, aiming at the man's back.

"Wait, don't shoot. It's me, Keegan."

It took a second to register but Raul kept his weapon trained as the man pivoted in the shadows. "Dammit, Keegan, what in the hell are you doing here?"

"I was close by. Heard the 911 call." He pointed to his car on the other side of the street.

"Are you sure about that? You didn't come because she blew you off?"

Keegan's eyes narrowed. "What the hell is that supposed to mean?" His eyes widened. "You can't seriously think that I'm the stalker?"

"You don't like to be turned down by women." He snatched Keegan's shirt. "And I know about those sexual harassment charges."

"Which were dismissed, you crazy bastard."

"They why were you skulking around the back?"

"I told you, I heard the call come in." Keegan snatched Raul's hand from him. "I checked the door and it was locked, so I ran around the side to see if a window was broken or another door jimmied. Nothing."

Raul climbed the steps two at a time, still skeptical. "Go around back, guard it, and I'll go in here."

Keegan nodded, bit out a curse, then ran around back, while Raul knocked. "Jenny, it's Raul. Open up!"

No response. He waited another second, listening for an intruder, a scream. But outside the storm raged and tossed pebbles across the drive, swirling leaves and twigs madly.

His chest heavy with fear, he jimmied the door and inched inside, his gun aimed. He scanned the entryway, the living room to the side but saw nothing.

"Jenny."

No response. God, she couldn't be dead. Please not dead. He couldn't stand it. Should have come over earlier. Not left her alone.

Deciding the killer might still be upstairs, he slowly crept up them, scanning the hallway, the empty bedroom to the left, then inching inside Jenny's. Darkness bathed the room, but through the shadows he noticed the bedcovers were rumpled, the lamp on the floor, the curtains flapping in the wind. Rain slashed the floor and he moved to the bathroom, his breath tight, terrified he'd find her body in the bathtub or shower.

Pain nearly immobilized him, but he moved on autopilot, checked the bathroom, the rest of the upstairs, but found nothing.

Fear clawed at him as he moved cautiously back down the stairs. He had to call it in, tell Keegan to canvass the area.

Then he noticed the office door to the left of the staircase. He'd never been inside it, but when he'd been here before it had been open. The door was closed now. Maybe the killer was holding her or hiding in waiting.

Slowly inching closer, he tried the door. Locked. Bracing his gun between his hands, he kicked the door open. It gave beneath his weight, but a chair was up against it and he shoved it aside.

"No!" A body jumped him, and he grabbed an arm,

then realized it was a woman's. Long hair brushed his face as he shook her. Jenny?

She had a hammer raised, but he gripped her hand and knocked it from her clutches, lowering his gun beside him at the same time.

"It's me, Raul! Stop fighting me, dammit."

She shrieked, then slowly relaxed as the truth registered. "Raul, God…"

"Shh, it's okay." He pulled her into his arms and she collapsed against him, sobbing uncontrollably.

"Someone was in the house," Jenny cried. "In my bedroom. He tried to strangle me."

"Are you hurt?" Raul stroked her back as he held her. "Talk to me, Jenny. Are you okay? Do you need a doctor?"

"No…no doctor," she whispered, although her voice sounded hoarse.

"What happened?" he asked against her ear.

"He tried to choke me."

He pulled back to look at her, examined her face and cursed at the blood. "Did you get a look at him?"

She shook her head, forcing herself to calm down. Raul was here. She was alive. He would protect her. "It was too dark. He must have cut the lights…."

"Bastard." He brushed a tear from her cheek. "Keegan is outside. Let me tell him to search the area."

She clutched his arm not wanting to let him go. "Raul—"

"Shh, it's okay. I'll be right back." She followed behind him to the door, and saw the deputy approach the porch. "She's in here," Raul shouted. "But she was attacked. Start canvassing the area, see if you find someone who looks suspicious. I'll phone for a crime-scene unit."

Keegan nodded and set off to comb the neighborhood while Raul rushed back to Jenny. She was trembling but her cries had quieted, and she wrapped her arms around herself trying to hold herself together physically and mentally.

"Jenny, are you sure you didn't see anything? A face, an outline? Was it your brother or that doctor?"

"I don't know. Not Bailey…" Her voice broke and she realized she sounded uncertain. "He had a scarf or something he used to try and strangle me."

"The Strangler," he said, although the MO was off slightly. The Strangler had drugged his other victims and had sex with them before he killed them. "Or it's possible someone who wanted us to think he was." He cursed. "How big was he?"

"I don't know." A shudder tore through her. "He had big hands. Rough."

"Did you detect an odor? Cigarettes? Cologne?"

"No…it happened so fast. I'm sorry, Raul. I was in bed and he appeared out of nowhere." Another shiver rippled up her spine at the memory of his hands around her throat, his weight on her, the force with which he'd struck her.

Lightning streaked the sky illuminating Raul's face which was chiseled in angry lines. "I'm calling CSI. He drugged the other girls, so they didn't fight back. If this is the same guy, he must be panicked, thinking we're closing in. Maybe in the fight you got some DNA from him, or he left a print this time."

If he was the same guy. Raul suspected a copycat, that her brother or Dr. Zovall might have attacked her. She didn't think Bailey would try to kill her, but earlier he'd lost it, had been violent. But the drugs and shock had triggered his violent reaction.

Now they knew the truth about what Dr. Zovall had done, it was possible he wanted to silence her.

"Raul, I want to call the hospital and check on Mom. Dr. Solaris said he'd beef up security and have them watch her room, but I'm worried."

He retrieved a flashlight from his car and shone it around for her to find the phone. She quickly dialed the hospital and relayed her concerns to the head of security. When she hung up, Raul was watching her, a feral gleam in his eyes.

"Dammit, Jenny, your forehead is bleeding," he growled. "Bastard hit you in the face, didn't he?"

"Yes, but I'm okay, really, Raul."

"You might need stitches." He pulled her to the kitchen, tore off some paper towels, dampened them, then blotted the blood from her forehead, insisting she lean over while he studied the depth and length of the gash.

The CSI team arrived, and Raul directed them to begin processing the crime scene.

Jenny prayed they found evidence, and that it didn't point to her brother.

FURY KNOTTED Raul's insides. Jenny had almost died tonight—he'd almost lost her. And he had no idea who had tried to kill her. Her brother? That crazy doctor?

Or the Strangler who'd already killed four women?

He'd vowed not to care for her, but the thought of finding her dead had ripped him apart inside. He should have gone with her to see her brother, but he'd been too busy protecting himself to realize that by not staying with her, he'd left her vulnerable.

It wouldn't happen again. From now on, he'd guard her day and night.

And he'd find the man who'd attacked her and make him pay.

He searched the outside of the house and discovered that a back window to the mudroom had been jimmied open. Keegan must have missed it.

He showed his findings to the crime-scene techs to dust for prints, although the rain would complicate forensics. Bushes lined the wall near the window, and he saw where they'd been crushed by a man's foot, but the rain had washed away any footprints. Still, he asked the team to search for indentations in the mud or muddy prints on the sidewalk out front.

The process took a couple of hours. Keegan returned, reporting that no one in the neighborhood had seen anyone suspicious.

How could this guy come in and out without being seen? Or had he? He must blend in so well that he didn't stick out as a suspect.

Finally the team finished, reporting they had a partial print on the stairwell that they'd check out. If they belonged to Bailey, it would be enough to bring him in for questioning. Maybe enough for a warrant to search wherever he was staying. See if he had a stash of silk panties hidden somewhere waiting to be used on another victim.

He found Jenny nursing a cup of hot tea, a bit of color returning to her cheeks, but the bruise on her forehead made fresh rage well up in his belly.

Keegan strode down the stairs. "Do you want me to stay here tonight, keep a watch out in case the guy returns?"

Raul shook his head. "No, I'll take care of Dr. Madden."

"Listen, Cortez, I don't mind taking a shift."

"I've got it covered," Raul snapped. "Just make sure the

trace is processed." He pulled Keegan outside out of Jenny's earshot. "And let me know if anything turns up with Dr. Zovall. Also, see if you can find Dr. Madden's brother, Bailey. I want him brought in for questioning."

Keegan arched a brow. "You think one of them is the Strangler?"

Raul shrugged. "The doc's too old to fit the profile, but he could be a copycat."

"And the brother?"

"A hothead, has alcohol and drug problems, and just found out some traumatic news."

Keegan whistled. "He blames Dr. Madden?"

"Could be he's taking his rage out on the messenger. Jenny had a confrontation with him earlier."

"I'll check in and keep you posted. Any idea where the brother might go?"

"According to his files, he has a substance abuse problem. Check the local bars and your snitches."

Keegan nodded. "I'll get right on it."

Raul thanked him, then returned to Jenny. She glanced up, her teacup still almost full, yet her hands were wrapped around it. She probably needed something stronger.

"Come on," he said gently. "We both know you won't sleep here tonight. Pack a bag. You're staying at my place."

Her gaze met his, questioning, uncertain.

"Please, Jenny. I need to make sure you're safe tonight. And the only way I can do that is to keep you with me."

She rose slowly but didn't argue. He followed her up the steps, and waited in the hall while she threw together an overnight bag. Five minutes later they were on their way to his duplex. Her shoulders were stiff, tension lining her face, her silence worrying him.

Guilt and anxiety knotted his insides. She had almost died tonight while he'd been protecting himself. A ploy that hadn't worked because when he'd thought that she might be dead, he'd wanted to join her.

Chapter Thirteen

Jenny helped others deal with grief, loss, shock, trauma and depression yet she felt herself slipping into the desolate grays, wondering what her purpose was in life. If she'd ever actually helped anyone. If she'd been so blinded to her own family's needs, how could she possibly understand a stranger's?

When Raul parked, she sat, shivering as if in a shell of a body, and listened to the drizzle of rain pelting the roof, to the wind howling from the heavens as if the innocent souls of the dead girls were screaming in pain at the injustice. Numb, she allowed him to assist her from the car.

And when he guided her to his bedroom, placed her bag on his bed and coaxed her to the bathroom, she did so on autopilot, oblivious to the world around her. She just needed to get warm. To forget.

He turned on the hot water and left her alone, and she undressed and stepped beneath the spray and closed her eyes. If only she could block out the truth about her mother, the horror of the man's hands around her throat, invading her bedroom, her space, his weight upon her as he squeezed the air from her lungs.

She soaped and scrubbed her body, wishing she could wash away the stench of violence that had invaded her life, but nothing she could do could erase reality.

Girls were being murdered in Savannah. One of her patients might be the killer, yet she was protecting him in the name of her job. Her mother might be in danger from a man Jenny had trusted with her life. And her baby brother was suffering, thinking he was the son of a rapist, his life spiraling out of control.

She had no idea which one of them had attacked her, but it was possible that any one of them was dangerous.

Finally the water grew cold, and she dried herself off. Shivering, she tugged on the cotton boxer shorts and camisole she'd brought to sleep in, then opened the bathroom door. Raul stood in the shadows, looking sexy and angry, the silhouette of a man in turmoil, and the most solid creature she'd ever known.

He led her to the bed, then thrust a glass into her hand. "I know you like wine, but I didn't have any. It's gin and tonic."

She drank it greedily, starving for anything to deaden the pain.

"Whoa, slow down." He cradled her hand and forced her to sip, not guzzle the drink. "I want to calm you, not make you sick."

"I can handle it," she whispered, her throat raw.

He rubbed a hand along the back of her neck, massaging the tension from her shoulders. "Oh, Jenny, you're always so strong. But it's okay to lean on me tonight."

Lean on him, when he hated what she did. When he was right all along. "No, you were right. I don't heal anyone, Raul. Just look at my family, they're falling apart."

Furious with herself for not seeing what was going on all these years, she went to the den and stared out through the screened sliding glass doors. Outside, the rain had slackened to a steady drizzle, and she heard the roaring of the waves crashing against the rocks, rolling in and out, never really going anywhere, just as she was.

He moved up behind her, and she felt his breath bathe her neck, felt his big masculine presence encompass her, his strength as he stroked her arms. "No, Jenny, I was wrong. You do help people, just by caring."

She spun around, ready to argue, hating herself and the fact that she'd failed the people she loved most. "My mother has been trapped in a prison made by her abuser all these years, crying out for me. My brother saw her raped, and now I realize his problems stem from that trauma. And what did I do? I read books, took classes, thought I knew it all, when I knew *nothing* about the people I loved the most."

"You were only a child when it happened, Jenny. You must have been hurting yourself, yet you grew up too quickly because you had to take care of everyone else." He tucked a strand of hair behind her ear, then caressed her face with her palm, his dark eyes meeting hers. "Who took care of you, though? No one."

"I can take care of myself."

"But you shouldn't have to," he said gruffly. "And you do help people, Jenny. You brought me back to life again."

Her heart pounded in her chest.

"You brought me back when I was dead inside because you cared." He traced a finger along her jaw. "Sometimes when we're that lost we don't even know we need a friend, yet you still tried to reach me. And you did."

She wanted to believe him, wanted him to hold her and obliterate the pain, to make her forget that a killer was out there and wanted her dead.

"Raul, I don't know who I am anymore. If I can go on."

He threaded his hand through her hair, his look so sexy that her legs nearly buckled. "You are the most beautiful woman I know."

Still, he'd pushed her away because of his dead wife. "You're still in love with Anita," she whispered.

Pain flashed in his eyes for a moment, and she regretted her words, but she didn't want him because he felt sorry for her.

His gaze met hers, intense, flickering with turmoil and other emotions. Hunger. Desire. Raw primal lust.

"The only woman in my head right now is you, Jenny." He dropped his forehead against hers, released a ragged breath that reeked of turmoil and a need so strong that it touched her deep inside.

"God forgive me, but you're the only woman I can think of right now. The one I want in my arms, in my bed, in my life."

She lifted a hand, caressed his strong jaw, felt the tension and unleashed passion building between them with each labored breath.

"It's okay to go on, Raul. To care about someone else."

"But I lost so much. I…don't think I could survive that kind of loss again." He brushed his lips against her cheek, teasing the corners of her mouth. "When I heard that 911 call and reached your place, when I couldn't find you, I—" his voice broke "—I thought I might find you dead…I wanted to die, too."

Tears filled her eyes, for him and his suffering. For the

need between them that was so overpowering she didn't care about anything else tonight but them.

RAUL HAD NEVER felt so raw and exposed, but he also couldn't hold back the truth. Jenny had a right to know that someone cared about her, that she wasn't alone.

She was the most unselfish person he'd ever met. Yes, he'd loved Anita, but he knew he'd put her on a pedestal, and that she had flaws. And caring for Jenny didn't diminish those feelings, because she understood that his heart had enough room for both of them.

The fact that they were so different, yet each woman touched some part of him meant he was one lucky son of a bitch. And he had been ready to throw that away.

He wanted Jenny, but whether they had a future was not the point. They needed to love each other tonight.

And he wanted to assuage her pain. He might not agree with all aspects of her job, but who was he to say it wasn't valuable when all he did was clean up the mess?

"Raul..."

His chest expanded with warmth when she said his name. Her tender touch on his face flamed his desires, heated his flesh with a yearning so strong that his blood sizzled in his veins.

He hadn't had a woman since his wife's death. Hadn't wanted one, but he wanted Jenny now. Not because she was a warm body and he was horny as hell, but because she was the sweetest, most loving person on earth.

"I want you, Jenny, but if you need to go to bed alone, I understand."

A small smile flickered in her eyes. "I do want to go to bed, Raul. But not alone."

His pulse kicked into double time as she took his hand and placed it on her breast. Her heart pounded beneath his palm, her breathing erratic as her chest rose and fell. Her nipples hardened, begging for his touch.

He lowered his head, flicked his tongue along the outer recesses of her mouth. She moaned and threaded her fingers into his hair, and he fused his mouth with hers, claiming her as he'd wanted to do from the first moment he'd laid eyes on her, when he knew it was wrong.

But nothing had ever felt so right.

She parted her lips, offering him entry, and he thrust his tongue inside, mimicking the way he wanted to join with her, the power of his thrusts growing faster and bolder as she ran her hands over his shoulders, clutching and clawing at his shirt.

She tore it off, and he flung it to the floor, frantic for more, to feel her bare breasts against his chest. A whisper of need fell from her lips as she ran her hands over his torso, and he trailed kisses along her neck and to her breasts. His hands held her weight in his palms, and her nipples stiffened, turgid and ready for his mouth. His sex hardened, swelling inside his pants to a painful throb, and he kneaded her, gently lowered the straps of her camisole, sucking her nipples through the thin cloth, wetting it with his greedy mouth.

She groaned his name and threw her head back, and he slid the camisole down, exposing her to his touch. But first he paused to appreciate her globes, flicking kisses along the mounds as she rocked her hips against his.

He trapped her nipple between his lips, tonguing it as he slid his hand between her thighs. She was damp, the cotton boxers sliding down easily to reveal her wet heat, the scent of her desire spurring his own. She kicked them off, and he pulled her closer, sliding two fingers between her legs and stroking her center.

He moved to her other breast, loving it the same way, thrusting his fingers inside her until she cried out for more. His body throbbing with hunger, he tore his mouth away. "To the bedroom," he mouthed against her neck.

She nodded, and rational sense interceded long enough for him to close and lock the sliding glass doors, then he picked her up and carried her to his bed. She tossed off the camisole, boldly offering him a view of her naked body in the faint light spilling in from the lamp in the den.

Already devoid of his shirt, he shoved his jeans down his thighs and quickly shed his clothing.

"Raul, you are the most powerful man I've ever known," she whispered as he knelt on the bed and pushed her legs apart.

She reached for him, but he wanted to give her this gift. So he closed his mouth over her heat, flicking his tongue along her damp thighs and into her center, using his tongue to love her the way he wanted to use his hard length. She moaned again, quivering as he licked and suckled her, then suddenly the tremors that had been building in her broke, and she shook with her release.

He rose above her, straddling her as he bent to nibble at her breasts again, then she reached for his sex. He stalled her hands, reached for a condom and rolled it on. Then he let her guide his aching length to her parted legs, then inside her, bracing himself to go slow. But she didn't seem to want slow. She arched her back, shoving her hips upward until he filled her completely, and he nearly lost control.

He wanted it to last, to be good for her, to make her

forget that men had brought her pain, that he wasn't like the ones who'd let her down. That he would never hurt her, that he'd protect her and give her pleasure instead.

She clutched his arms and he kissed her again, deeply, his passion rising as her muscles squeezed around him, and she twined her legs around his waist. He slid his hands under her hips, angled her so he could drive himself deeper, and she begged for him to move faster, not to stop. His hunger spiraled out of control, the animal inside him surfacing until he forgot where they were, only that he'd waited for this moment, needed to grind faster and deeper.

She gripped his hips, holding him firmly between her thighs, urging him on with whispered sighs until he felt as if he was coming apart. Just as the strains of his resistance faltered and he teetered on the brink of orgasm, she cried his name and began to quiver again. Sensations so powerful he couldn't speak shot through him as his own release came.

Her name escaped his lips on a tormented passion-glazed shout, and he clutched her close to him, moved by the intense pleasure of joining his body with hers, of feeling her alive in his arms, and knowing that he had eased her pain and brought her pleasure.

JENNY CURLED into Raul's arms, for the first time in her life feeling safe and cared for. Somewhere in the back of her brain, a warning bell clamored, reminding her not to make too much of their lovemaking, that Raul still carried baggage and that one night didn't mean they had a future together. But she shushed the voice, unable to bear the thought of him leaving her yet. She needed his arms tonight, his lips, his body. But more than that, she needed to believe that her life held the promise of happiness, not just the endless parade of dysfunction and sadness. That she might have a chance at a family who trusted and loved and nurtured each other.

And a man who would never desert her.

BAILEY WALKED and walked in circles around Savannah, dipping into one bar after the other, trying desperately to drown the voice hammering inside his head.

It's your fault Dad left. You told him that Mommy was in bed with another man.

It's your fault your mother has been ill all these years. You were too scared to see what was really happening.

It's your fault she's lived in that bed of horror like a damned vegetable.

Yet he still hated her. Hated her for leaving him, for not being strong enough to fight the doctor, for not telling somebody what was going on.

Hated her for sinking into that empty shell and not loving him.

He'd needed her just like he'd needed his daddy.

But both of them had left him.

And now he'd lost Jenny, too. He'd seen the look in her eyes when she'd told him the truth about their mother. She'd thought he was worthless for a long time, but she still hadn't totally abandoned him.

But he'd gone too far tonight. Because she blamed him for breaking up the family. For not saving their mother.

Gulping back another scotch, he savored the hot burn of the booze sliding down his throat. He gripped the bar's edge, waving to the bartender for another. He needed something to soothe the blinding rage chewing his insides. That and the damn guilt that was more painful than any of the beatings he'd taken at the hands of loan sharks when he hadn't paid them.

Yet relief refused to come.

He had to do something. His heart pumping, he tossed down the drink, threw some cash on the counter, then stalked outside. He had to see his mother. Find out if Jenny had been lying.

Find that doctor.

And if he had abused his mother, had forced himself on her, Bailey would kill him.

Chapter Fourteen

The ringing of his cell phone dragged Raul back to reality at 5:00 a.m. Girls were dead and another might be dying. He had to go back to work.

He dropped a kiss on Jenny's forehead, then left her sleeping peacefully, his jaw tightening all over again at the sight of the bruise on her forehead and neck.

He couldn't let this bastard get away with what he'd done or hurt Jenny again.

The phone jangled again, and he grabbed it and walked into the kitchen to make coffee.

"Cortez."

"It's Black. The IT guys found something on the computers. It might be a lead, Raul, so I want you here to discuss it with them."

"I'll be right there." He scrubbed a hand over his chin. "Do you have that warrant for Dr. Madden's files?"

"Yes, you can pick it up when you come in."

Jenny wouldn't like it, but she was right. He had to do what he had to do. Just as he had to locate that brother of hers and put him under the microscope.

By the time he dressed, Jenny was rolling over, her sleepy gaze meeting his. "Where are you going?"

He walked over, traced a finger along her jaw. He wanted to crawl back in bed and make love to her again. "To meet the captain. The tech team may have a lead from the victims' computers."

"Let me dress and I'll go with you."

He shook his head. "No one knows you're here. Stay in bed and rest, Jenny. You need it." He touched the bruise on her forehead. "And you deserve it."

"You'll come back?"

He nodded gravely as the pain returned to her eyes. He wanted to erase it. Wanted her again, bad. "As soon as I can."

Tearing his gaze away from her bare breasts peeking from beneath the covers, he stepped back. He had to go now. He had a case to solve, and if her brother was involved, he'd have to arrest him.

Then he'd lose her because she'd hate him for it.

JENNY FELT BEREFT and lonely as Raul walked out the door. She told herself that he'd return. That he hadn't left forever.

But the emptiness throbbed inside her, along with reality. Somebody wanted her dead.

She closed her eyes and tried to go back to sleep, but images of the man attacking her the night before drove her from bed. Memories of her confrontation with Bailey followed, along with the truth about Dr. Zovall. She wanted to confront him in person, ask him how he could have abused his patients in such a way.

And she needed to figure out why she had trusted him so blindly, even allowed him to mentor her into studying psychiatry, when he'd been a fraud.

When he had destroyed her family.

The anger she'd fought last night surfaced with a vengeance. She had to visit her mother. Assure her that she was finally aware now of what this horrible man had done to her. That she would stick by her and do everything in her power to support her during recovery.

Adrenaline pumping, she dressed quickly, then phoned for a taxi. While she waited, she scribbled Raul a note saying she'd be at the hospital. First she had to shower and clean up, though. After visiting with her mother, she had an appointment with her support group for sexual deviants. Not smart to do that with the scent of Raul's lovemaking on her skin.

When the taxi arrived, she locked Raul's door, then asked the cab driver to take her home. For a moment she hesitated in the cab, reluctant to go inside. Last night she'd nearly died here.

But she refused to let some psycho drive her from her own house, or to be trapped by fear. If she did, she'd be no better off than the patients she treated.

Still, entering her dark house made a shiver ripple up her spine, the reason she'd left with Raul the night before screaming through her mind. The smell of fear and danger permeated the air, and fingerprint dust dotted the surfaces of the doors, windows, phone, everywhere she looked.

At least Raul had had someone turn the power back on, and she flipped on the lights as she slowly inched her way through the house. She should have let Raul come with her, check it out before she returned.

But she couldn't allow herself to grow too dependent.

Her cell phone rang, and she grabbed it, frantic that another girl had been killed. Or maybe they'd located Dr. Zovall.

She checked the number on the caller box. Her service. "Dr. Madden speaking."

"Dr. Madden, Dr. Solaris asked me to call you," a male voice said. "Your mother has been upset all night and is asking for you."

"I'll be right there." Jenny's heart pounded as she hung up, threw the locks on the doors and jumped into the shower. Dr. Solaris was weaning her mother from some of the drugs. Had she become more coherent? Able to finally relay the details of her abuse?

She hurriedly dressed, made a pot of coffee and slugged one down. It was still dark outside as she rushed to her car. If she hurried, she could make it for her mother's morning bath. Maybe she could brush her hair...

In the garage she fumbled with her keys, jumped in her car, then pressed the door lock button, but just as she did, the hushed whisper of a breath bathed her neck. Panic seized her throat as a man grabbed her from behind. The sharp jab of a needle pricking her skin sent ice-cold fear through her.

The fear lasted only a second before darkness descended and she disappeared into it.

RAUL WATCHED as the techies showed him how they had traced the MySpace accounts, noting the various servers and the difficulties in tracking down the real identities and addresses.

"We discovered a common thread," Edgar, one of the team said. "Although the addies say different, and the guy used various names when contacting the victims, the e-mails originated from one computer source."

Raul stared in shock as the information spieled onto the screen. The address: Jenny Madden's house.

"What the hell?"

Captain Black frowned. "That's Dr. Madden's." He turned to Raul. "Who had access to her computer?"

Raul's mind raced. "At work, maybe her secretary but I'm sure Jenny's files are password protected."

"What about her house?"

He twisted his mouth in thought, then grimaced. "Her brother."

"You know where he is?"

"We're looking for him now."

"Anyone else?"

Raul thought back. "She's had a worker there doing renovations, but he's an old man. He doesn't fit the profile."

"What if he's in disguise?" Black asked. "I mean, what do you really know about this man?"

Raul scowled. He'd go with the brother for the crime but better to check every avenue. "Nothing."

Black stared at him for a long moment. "Give me his name and I'll run it."

"His name is Ralph Martin."

"Thanks."

Raul had been chewing over the profile, Jenny's family history, the abusive doctor. He was missing something; he couldn't put his finger on it.

"I want to look at Jenny's patient files." Then another thought struck him. "What if one of Jenny's Atlanta patients stole Machete's ID and followed her here?"

"A disgruntled patient she left behind?" Black said, jumping onto Raul's train of thought. "Then Jenny might be the center of it."

"God." He swiped a clammy hand over his neck. "I need Jenny's records from Atlanta. And I need to talk to her. Maybe she can give us a name." His heart pounded. "He's already tried to kill her once. He won't stop until he succeeds."

BAILEY WANTED TO KILL Dr. Zovall so bad he could taste his blood.

If the doctor knew the cops were on to him, he'd protect himself. He might come after Bailey's mother to keep her quiet.

Smiling at his genius thoughts, he retrieved his cell phone and looked up Doc Zovall's number. He punched it in but received the bastard's voice mail.

Zovall had always told him to call him if he needed anything. The old man had not only pretended to be his friend, but had tried to play daddy.

Because he was his father?

"Hey, Doc," he said. "It's Bailey." He hesitated, let his voice crack, aiming for drama. "Listen, Jenny told me some weird stuff this new doctor said. I'm on my way to see Mom now because I don't believe it."

He cut the call, leaving on that note, and hoping the doc would take the bait. Patting the knife he kept in his boot, he staggered toward a cab and waved it down. He'd see his mother himself. Ask her what happened.

Then he'd wait on the doc to show. And he'd make him pay for stealing his mother.

JENNY WAS COLD. Bone-deep shivering cold. Her head hurt. Her stomach roiled. And her limbs felt weighted down as she struggled to move them.

Where was she? And what had happened?

A frisson of fear danced through her head as memory slowly interceded. She'd gone home to change, but someone had assaulted her.

The fear expanded to full-blown panic. The stalker... he'd been waiting for her in the garage, had known she'd return to claim her car and he'd have her alone. Then he'd grabbed her.

And taken her where?

She tried to move again, but her hands were tied, her feet bound together at the ankles. The floor below her was cold and hard—a basement maybe? Was she in a house? Near the beach? In Savannah? Or had he driven her out of town, so far no one would find her?

No, the other girls had been found near Savannah. The photos of their dead bodies rose to haunt her. Would she be next?

No…she couldn't die. Had too much to look forward to. Her mother might finally recover. And Raul…he'd said he'd return. He'd make love to her again. That was something to live for.

She sucked in a deep breath, trying desperately to calm her nerves. The air smelled stale, musty, the stench of dust and mold clogging her nostrils. She opened her eyes and searched the darkness, but wherever she was, was so black that she could see only shadows. A sob built in her throat, but she willed herself to control it. She had to stay calm. Figure out where she was. Stall so Raul could find her.

Raul…did he even know she was missing? How long had she been unconscious?

And who had her? Was he here now, watching her? Laughing at the fear in her labored breathing?

Was it one of her patients?

Chapter Fifteen

Raul's gut suddenly started churning with that same sick feeling he'd had the day Mulstein had been let out on bail.

The day he'd lost his wife and child.

Jenny.

God.

He prayed his instincts were wrong. But there were too many variables. Too many suspects unaccounted for.

The doctor who'd hurt Jenny's mother hadn't been found. Neither had her volatile brother. And then there was the list of patients at CIRP and Atlanta.

He had to talk to Jenny.

Sweat beading on his upper lip, he phoned his home, pacing the captain's office. One ring. Two. Three. Four. No answer.

She might not answer your phone, idiot.

Right. He tried her cell phone, and let it ring and ring until her voice mail picked up. "Jenny, it's Raul. Call me now. I need to know you're okay."

Captain Black strode in seconds later. "Fox is tracking down Dr. Madden's practice in Atlanta."

Raul nodded, his pulse racing with nervous energy.

"Jenny didn't answer the phone. I'm going to check my house, see if she's there."

Black nodded. "I'll let you know what we find out from Atlanta."

"And I want to know as soon as you track down Jenny's brother."

"Of course. Take the warrant and get those files on Dr. Madden's patients."

Raul stuffed the warrant inside his jacket pocket, then hurried out of the precinct to his car. The sun was trying to bleed through the ominous gray clouds but failing miserably. He maneuvered the streets easily, the morning traffic not in full swing yet, and made it to his place in just under ten minutes. Throwing the car into Park, he hit the ground running.

Surely he'd find Jenny still in bed, sleeping peacefully. He was just being paranoid. Fate wouldn't be so cruel as to let this killer find her, not in his own damn house.

But what if he'd been watching them?

The door was locked. A good sign. And he didn't see any indication it had been tampered with. Taking a deep breath, he shoved open the door, shouting Jenny's name as he dashed to the bedroom.

The breath lodged in his throat. The bed was empty.

Dammit.

Praying she was in the shower, he shoved open the bathroom door but saw nothing, except the towels where they'd bathed the night before. Memories of loving her crashed back. He wanted to hold her again. Feel her beneath him crying his name in pleasure.

Panic threatened, but he assured himself she'd probably gone to the hospital. She'd been worried about her mother. He called the hospital, but her secretary said she hadn't shown yet.

He leaned against the door, forcing himself to think like a cop not a man who might have just lost someone very important to him. What would Jenny do first?

Go home to shower and dress.

But she'd need a ride. Why hadn't she called him?

Because she was independent. Had taken care of herself for so long she didn't lean on anyone. And even though he'd made love to her, had promised her protection, he'd never spoken about a long-term relationship.

Because he'd been scared senseless.

He was even more terrified now. Terrified he'd lose her. Terrified that he'd made a huge mistake by protecting himself instead of allowing himself to love her.

Guilt mingled with cold fear, and he raced back to the bedroom, glanced at the nightstand, then the kitchen and spotted a note. Exhaling in relief, he picked it up and read it:

> Raul, I have to see Mom. Took a cab home. Will call
> you later. Thank you for last night.
> Jenny.

Crushing the note in one hand, he raced back to his car and sped toward her house. The first rays of sun splintered through the clouds, yet thunder rumbled in the distance, and a few lone cars had ventured out. He bypassed them, sailed over the bridge and maneuvered the streets in Savannah until he reached her house. Again he threw the car into Park and hurried up the steps. The door was locked, and he knocked, punching the doorbell repeatedly.

No answer.

His heart began to race again, the reprieve from her note evaporating as he noticed that the detached garage door was open. Pulling his gun from his holster, he inched toward the door, trained and ready to shoot should there be trouble. His heart stopped when he spotted Jenny's purse on the garage floor beside her car door. Her keys lay near the back tire, the contents of her purse scattered across the concrete, droplets of blood splattered against the pale paint of her car.

His legs nearly buckled as the truth hit him.

Jenny had been abducted.

BAILEY SLIPPED into the hospital, easing his way along the corridors until he found the stairs. This early, the staff seemed lean, the place quiet. He'd seen a security guard on the way inside, but he'd waited until the guard turned the other way, then ducked past him.

He crept along the hall, slipping into the bathroom when another nurse came around the bend, then waited until she'd crossed to the nurses' station down the hall to dash into his mother's room.

He hesitated when he saw his mother lying in the bed, her graying hair stark against the pristine white sheets. She was sleeping, looking peaceful, and his heart throbbed with broken memories.

Had he misjudged her all those years ago? Was she being raped, crying for help, and he'd misinterpreted the situation?

Tears leaked down his eyes and dripped off his chin. He'd hated her most of his life. Hadn't visited her the last year at all.

Hurt and anger and grief for losing his family bombarded him, and he dropped down into the chair, lay his head on the bed beside her hand and began to sob.

That hatred toward her had spilled over into his entire life, had ruined everything he'd touched. And he'd been wrong...

Now that same hatred burned like acid in his gut, except it was aimed at that bastard doctor.

How could his mother forgive him for what he'd done? And how could she love him if he was that monster's son?

Suddenly he felt her fingers slide over his head, felt her ruffling his hair as she had done when he was a small boy. He lifted his head slightly and looked up into her eyes. They looked clearer now than they had the last time he'd seen her. And held a softness that broke his heart.

"Bailey...it's going to be okay, son," she whispered.

He nodded, then squeezed her hand. It would now, because he would make it right.

She smiled and he huddled closer, taking solace as she stroked his hair. They sat there for a long time, her soothing him, him whispering that he was sorry, that he would make up for the past.

"I love you, Bailey. I always have."

"I love you, too, Mom." Emotions hung in his throat, along with the question he didn't want to ask. Was he her rapist's son? How could she love him then?

In the hall the rattle of shoes and carts broke the silence. Wiping the tears from his face, he pushed to his feet and went into the bathroom to wash his face.

"Don't go, Bailey," she said softly. "Stay and talk."

"I'm not leaving, Mama," he said. "I just want to clean up."

She nodded, and he stepped inside and turned on the water, disgusted with himself. He looked terrible, bleary-eyed from too much booze and lack of sleep. And he smelled like scotch and sweat.

His mother deserved better. He'd go back to the hotel,

shower. Find a way to get his life back. Atone to his mother and Jenny for all the trouble he'd caused.

Behind him in the hospital room, the door to the hallway screeched open. One of the nurses most likely. But he peeked through the edge of the door and gripped the sink edge as Dr. Zovall walked into the room.

Dressed in surgical garb, he might not have identified him, but Bailey knew the man well and recognized his gait. The cocky son of a bitch.

His mother made a whimpering sound, and Bailey saw the doctor raise a needle in one hand. Zovall had drugged his mother and taken advantage of her in her incapacitated state.

Today it would stop.

Reaching inside his boot, he retrieved his knife. Holding his breath, he waited until the doctor had neared his mother's bed, then he sprang from the bathroom and grabbed him around the neck. With a growl of pure rage, he thrust the blade to the man's throat.

He started to slice into Zovall's skin and drain the life from him, then his mother screamed.

RAUL'S PULSE RACED. As soon as he obtained that list of Jenny's patients, he'd call in officers to track them down. If one of them had Jenny, he'd use every available source to find him and save her.

Images of what the man might be doing to her tormented him as he arrived at the hospital, but his cell phone rang, and he stamped them down. "Detective Cortez."

"Cortez, this is Black. The head of security just called from CIRP and said Dr. Zovall showed up in Mrs. Madden's room, and Jenny's brother was there. He tried to kill the doctor but the mother screamed and the guard intervened."

"I'm at the hospital now. I'll talk to the brother."

He hung up and raced up the steps, his pulse clamoring. He didn't want to think that Bailey would hurt his own sister but who knew how disturbed the young man really was?

Raul would extract the truth from him if he had to beat it out of him.

A security guard met him in the hallway. "Dr. Zovall was stabbed but he'll live. The doctors are stitching him up, then you can have him. Bailey Madden is in the main security office. We were holding him until you showed up."

Raul hurried down the corridor, turned left, then found the office.

He heard Bailey shouting from behind the door. "He was going to kill my mother. He had it coming."

"Just chill out and calm down, kid," one of the guards ordered.

Raul couldn't blame Bailey for his actions. He'd do the same thing if someone abused his mother. He pushed open the doors and saw Bailey handcuffed to a metal desk, a guard on each side.

Rage and fear flashed in the young man's eyes when he spotted Raul. "I should have known they'd call you."

"You listen to me, you punk, you'd better straighten up right now." Raul gave him a cold look. "Your sister is missing and I need to know if you've seen her."

Bailey's face went stark white. "What do you mean, she's missing?"

"I went to her house, and found her purse contents scattered on the floor beside her car. She wasn't inside, hasn't shown up at work, hasn't contacted her service." He shoved his face in Bailey's. "Last night someone broke into her house and tried to strangle her."

"No…God…no…" Bailey tried to jump up but the handcuff jerked him back down, and he cursed.

"Bailey, you were upset with your sister yesterday," Raul said. "She told you about Zovall and you went ballistic, didn't you?"

"Wouldn't you?" Pure hatred glittered in the boy's eyes, but there was pain, as well.

Raul's heart clenched, but he had to have answers. "Did you try to hurt her last night?"

"Hell, no," Bailey snarled. "I went and got drunk…then I decided to visit my mother." His voice broke, choking with emotions. "I showed up here and then that crazy bastard came in. He was going to drug my mother again."

"You have a MySpace account," Raul said. "You set it up through your sister's computer."

He sat up again, jerking his hand to try to free himself. "I did no such thing."

Raul scowled. "You didn't use her computer to set up an account?"

"I said I didn't," Bailey shouted. "Besides, what's that got to do with my sister missing?"

Raul knew the kid had had a lot dumped on him in a short time. If he had nothing to do with Jenny's abduction, this was going to be a blow. "We think the Savannah Strangler found his victims through MySpace accounts."

Bailey began to tremble so hard he collapsed into the chair, then dropped his head into his hands. "You think that psycho killer has Jenny?"

Raul clenched his hands into fists. "I'm not sure, but it looks like a distinct possibility."

"God, not Jenny…" Tears filled Bailey's eyes. "You have to find her, man. I…I have to tell her I'm sorry."

"Sorry for what?" Raul ground out.

"For Mom," he choked on a sob. "And for being a loser brother." He looked up at Raul, chin quivering. "Please save her, Detective. Jenny can't be dead. Mom and I both need her."

And so did he, but he refrained from confessing it out loud. He explained that they had to take him into custody for assaulting the doctor, then phoned for a uniform to pick up Bailey. Raul was certain, though, that the charges wouldn't stick. Still, Bailey was a loose cannon, and he wanted him contained until they found his sister.

Raul wouldn't allow himself to even contemplate that they wouldn't.

JENNY STRUGGLED against the bindings, twisting her hands and arms, desperate to escape before her abductor returned. She rubbed the ropes against the floor until her skin was raw and blood trickled down her hands onto her palms. Tears threatened, but she blinked them back in the darkness, wishing she could see where she was. Wishing she'd waited on Raul.

What was he doing now? Did he know she was missing? Was he tearing things apart looking for her?

So far, she hadn't seen her attacker's face. Had no idea if he was one of her patients or a stranger. She had to climb inside his head, find out the reason he'd abducted her. The reason he'd killed those women.

If she could get him to talk, she could stall.

But she was in no hurry to face him.

Biting back a whimper of fear, she wrestled with the bindings again, each moment that ticked by intensifying her terror. Memories of the past few days crashed back.

Visiting that first crime scene, seeing Judy Benson's blank eyes staring up at her in death. Then Eleanor's. The vulgar position of their bodies. How she'd wanted to cover the girl while they photographed her.

They'd do the same to her....

No. She couldn't think like that. Had to stay strong, stay positive. Couldn't let fear overpower her.

Forcing thoughts of the bodies into the far recesses of her mind, she focused on recalling pleasant memories. Memories of her and Bailey before their father walked out. Of Christmas, tearing open brightly wrapped presents, and opening the toys Santa had left for them under the tree. The doll she'd wanted when she was five. The tricycle for Bailey. The doctor's kit when she was six, the baseball glove for Bailey.

Then everything had fallen apart.

Of course, now she knew that it had all started years before that.

And poor Bailey...he blamed himself. He needed help, needed her. What would happen if she didn't survive? Would he straighten up and take care of their mother?

The bad memories pressed in again, weighting down her chest, and her breathing became heavy. She shoved them away again, thought of Raul. His strong face, the determination in his eyes when he was working.

The heat when he'd made love to her.

She latched on to the blissful comfort of his arms around her, reminded herself that Raul was smart. Strong. That he wouldn't give up until he found her.

And when her abductor returned, she'd play his game and string him out. Serial killers murdered because they wanted attention. She'd give it to him. Let him tell his story.

And hope that Raul found her in time before the Strangler added her to his list of victims.

RAUL HAD TO THINK like a detective, not allow his personal emotions to interfere. Hopefully the crime unit he'd asked to sweep Jenny's garage would find something. And maybe the Atlanta files would provide the answer.

What about the MySpace account? If Bailey hadn't used Jenny's computer to set it up, who the hell had?

Someone who'd tapped into her system, someone who knew a lot about computers? He phoned the tech team and asked them to follow up, see if they could trace another connection.

He raced up to Jenny's office to confiscate her patient files. Maybe one of them had computer expertise. He was grasping but he had to follow every lead.

When he explained that Jenny was missing, her receptionist paled. "Oh, my goodness, you don't think that stalker has her, do you?"

"I don't know, but I need her patient files *asap.*"

Her hand trembled as she examined the warrant. "You think one of Dr. Madden's patients is the Strangler?"

"Again, I can't say, but we need to check those files."

She nodded, stood and went to retrieve the list. It took her several minutes to print it out, and she gave him a weary look when she handed it over. "Dr. Madden won't like this."

"I know," he said through gritted teeth. He could put up with her anger, but not losing her. "Better that than death."

Her eyes widened and she sank back into her chair, shaking.

"I'm going to use her office to look through them." She

didn't bother to argue, and he strode to Jenny's desk and spread out the list. His head hurt as he began to weed through the names, striking off all the female patients first, then focusing on individuals Jenny had flagged as violent or ones with criminal pasts. Jamal Rakely's name stuck out along with Clyde Anson's. And one more, a guy named Carl Huggins, who had an obsession with silk and satin. Jenny had noted that he'd commented about tying women up, punishing them if they didn't obey him. Carl also worked with computers.

He punched in the number for the precinct and spoke to his partner. "Keegan, I've got three names. I want patrol cars sent out and these guys picked up for questioning." He listed the names and addresses and Keegan agreed to take care of it.

Raul heard the captain's voice in the background. "Captain wants to talk to you."

"Yeah. Put him on."

"Cortez, we got a hit on that name, Bobby Machete."

"You know who stole the ID?"

"No, but he owned a cabin here in Savannah, out by the marsh. You want to meet me out there."

"I'm on my way." Raul jammed the files under his arm and jogged toward the door. Black gave him the address and he ran down the steps to his car, his heart racing. He didn't know how long this psycho had held his victims before he'd killed them, but every second counted.

Traffic was beginning to pick up as he sped toward the marshland, and he turned on his siren to bypass the worst. A few drops of rain splattered the windshield, the scent of the marsh more pungent with the humidity. A boat puttered to life and drifted through the inlet, a fisherman out for an early-morning trip. Life looked normal, with people heading to work, tourists emerging, joggers and walkers filling the sidewalks. Life as usual…yet the world was off-kilter. The women in Savannah had been in danger and still were.

And the one who mattered to him the most was in the madman's hands.

Five minutes later he veered into a short driveway leading to a rundown shack that had seen better days. Bobby Machete had bought this place?

It was set off from the others around it, desolate, isolated. A hideaway or a hideout?

A knot of fear settled in his belly. If he'd brought the women here to kill them, no wonder no one had seen or heard anything.

The captain hadn't arrived yet, and Raul knew he should wait for backup, but Jenny might be inside. And God knew what this sicko was doing to her…

Pulling his weapon from his holster, he eased through the overgrown sea oats encompassing the property, and inched up to a side window. He glanced inside, but the place was dark and appeared empty. Shag carpet, ancient furniture and dust told him the place was deserted.

Frustration clogged his throat—he wanted Jenny to be here. Wanted the killer so he could end his sorry life.

What if he'd strangled Jenny already and was en route now to dump her body? The images of the other girls haunted him, but he quickly banished them. He had to focus. Not give up. Find her.

There might be evidence inside.

Slowly he circled the house looking for signs of inhabitants and checking the windows, but saw nothing. He jiggled the back door and it screeched open. The wood floors creaked as he made his way inside. The kitchen held a rickety Formica table, sagging cabinets and smelled musty. It also smelled of coffee.

Someone had been here recently.

Lungs tight, he moved through the kitchen to the den, his weapon trained in case of an attacker. Nothing.

Paint peeled from the door, and he reached for the rusty doorknob and turned it, his breath frozen in his lungs.

Would he find Jenny inside?

Chapter Sixteen

Raul clenched his weapon tighter as he slowly opened the door, bracing himself for an attack. But when he opened the door, his heart sank.

No Jenny.

Panic tore at him, his imagination running wild. Had she been here?

The bed had been disturbed. The covers mussed. Droplets of blood tinged the floor.

Would the blood match Jenny's?

God, what had the bastard done to her?

He'd drugged the other women, had sex with them, then strangled them....

A car engine sounded outside, and Raul eased back through the house, hoping it was the guy who'd stolen Machete's identity. But his captain exited from the unmarked car and Raul met him at the door.

"No one inside, but there are signs someone has been here recently."

"I'll get a crime unit here." Captain Black phoned in the request as he followed Raul inside the house. They searched the rooms, desk in the den, kitchen drawers for anything that might indicate where the man might be or where he might have taken Jenny.

No notes, scraps of paper with scribbled addresses. No maps. No brochures. Nothing.

He moved back to the bedroom, his heart clenching at the blood droplets, then checked the closet. There were no clothes inside, no slacks or shoes, no rope…

Was the man staying someplace else?

On the top shelf he noticed a wooden box, and he took it down and opened it.

Silk panties.

Not the kind that were used to strangle the victims, but four pairs in different sizes and styles.

The police had wondered about the girls' underwear, if it had been the man's trophy.

They were right. These had probably belonged to the victims….

His heart raced. The killer had stolen them for himself, meaning he might not have used gloves when he handled them. Maybe they'd get prints or DNA.

Black shouted his name and Raul carried the box to the second bedroom to show him what he found. "The girls' underwear…we were right, it was his trophy."

"And look what I found." With his gloved hand, the captain indicated a shoebox, and Raul peered down into it.

"Tapes," Black said. He held up one and showed Raul the label.

"Judy Benson." Raul's blood ran cold as he noticed the names on the other tapes. One tape for each of the girls.

"Holy hell," he muttered. "You think he taped the rape and murder?"

Black shrugged. "We'll have to check them out to know for sure. And if he did, we might get a face."

Another possibility sent a shudder through Raul. "Or he might have been stalking the women and taped them beforehand."

"It's possible he set up cameras in their homes," Black suggested.

Raul cursed and punched in the number for the crime unit, hoping they were still at Jenny's house.

Jordan, one of the techs, answered on the third ring.

"Listen, we found tapes of the Strangler victims. Check and see if there are hidden cameras inside Dr. Madden's house."

Jordan agreed, and Raul hung up, a knot in his stomach, his throat thick with rage and fear. Had this psycho been taping Jenny? Spying on her in her house when she had no idea he was watching?

And what was he doing to her now? Taping her while she struggled to escape him? While he took her against her will?

While he killed her?

HE WANTED JENNY, had wanted her from the first moment he'd seen her. From the first time he'd walked into her office and she'd spoken his name.

That voice...so husky soft and seductive. And her eyes, they had been so kind. So understanding. So loving and innocent.

Not like his mother's. That cold bitch who'd thrown him away like a sack of garbage. Tossed him into that orphanage where he'd been treated like nothing.

He'd scrapped and fought his way through, a mere

number in a host of unwanted. An invisible kid the regular kids in school laughed at.

Snotty-nosed, poor little boy with no family, they'd taunted.

His temper had shut them up though. And as he grew older, he'd learned to be charming. Had cleaned himself up so the women even wanted him.

But they never stayed. They always left.

Because they were sluts. Not good girls like Jenny.

Anger zinged through every inch of his flesh, though, as he realized the truth. Jenny wasn't good, either.

She had deserted him, too, when she'd come to Savannah. Then she'd shacked up with that cop like a commoner. Had forgotten him and invited more men into her office.

He would make her pay for that. Nobody left him, not anymore.

Not ever again.

But he would have her first. Finally.

He popped in the tape from her house and hit Play, then relaxed on the bed as he watched her enter her house. She rubbed her temple and walked to the kitchen, then poured herself a glass of wine. Then she carried it to her bedroom. Excitement shot through him, and his body hardened.

Slowly she peeled off her clothes, the silk blouse, skirt, shoes, down to her underwear. The black lace bra containing her breasts made his mouth water. Then she flicked the clasp, and her heavy globes sprang free, her nipples tightening as the air hit them. He visibly gulped in a breath, squirming with anticipation.

Nude now except for that pair of satin panties that barely covered her precious secrets, he licked his lips. He itched for release as she slid them down her slender thighs and kicked them off. Groaning, he forced his hands to his side, refusing to touch himself. He wanted to be inside her when he enjoyed his release.

His excitement built as she walked naked to the bathroom and filled the tub with bubbly water. Bringing her wine with her, she sank down inside the hot water and moaned as the bubbles dotted her flesh. He imagined her moaning like that when he was inside her. Imagined her calling his name in a sultry whisper as he made love to her.

And her screams when he wrapped a pair of panties around her neck and choked the life from her.

RAUL'S PHONE TRILLED as he secured the evidence in Captain Black's police car. "Detective Cortez."

Hoping for another lead, he quickly connected the call. "Detective, this is Sergeant Humphries from the Atlanta PD. Dr. Ragan, a former partner with Dr. Jenny Madden, phoned and told me you guys were looking into a man named Bobby Machete."

Impatience tightened Raul's mouth. "Yeah, we believe the man who has been strangling women here in Savannah stole Machete's ID. What do you know about him?"

"We investigated his death, and although we didn't find anything conclusive, we suspected that he might have been murdered."

"Did you have any suspects?"

"One. A mental patient named Felix Brainard. Like Machete, Brainard was a patient of Dr. Madden's."

"Do you know where Brainard is now?"

"No. We didn't have anything concrete to hold him on and had to cut him loose."

"Do you have an address?"

"No. According to his landlord, he left town a couple of months ago but didn't leave any forwarding information."

Raul's pulse was racing. Brainard might be their killer. "Can you fax a photo of him to our precinct, along with any other information you have on him?"

"Sure. Dr. Ragan released his medical file, so I'll send those as well."

"Did he have any family or friends that he might go to?" Raul asked.

"Guy had no friends or family to speak of. He grew up in an orphanage. But according to Dr. Ragan, he'd just discovered his father's identity. He might have left town to track him down."

"What's his name?" Raul asked.

"Ralph Martin."

Raul's chest heaved for air. Martin, the old man who was working on Jenny's house. His son was Brainard...

"Thank you, Sergeant."

He hung up and spun toward Black, quickly relaying the information.

"I'll wait on CSI to sweep this place. I want to know whose blood that is," Black said. "Then I'll take the underwear and tapes to the station for processing."

Raul nodded, adrenaline pumping. "I'll find Martin. He doesn't know we're on to him," Raul said. "And he should be at Jenny's this morning. The Atlanta PD is faxing over info on this Brainard guy."

Old man or not, if Martin had helped his son murder these women or covered for him, Raul would force him to talk.

The clock was ticking.

THE DOOR SCREECHED OPEN, the sound heavy metal against concrete, and Jenny cringed. She was about to meet her abductor.

She clenched her hands, yanking against the ropes for the hundredth time, willing them to break and set her free. At least then she'd have a fighting chance.

But no, her attacker wanted her afraid, vulnerable—to exert his power over her.

Somehow she had to use that against him. Because needing that power meant he was weak inside, broken.

Footsteps shuffled across the floor, the dank smell mingling with perspiration and her own fear. He moved closer, his figure a lone darkness in the midst of the black abyss of the room. His breathing sounded choppy, labored. Nervous or excited?

Bile rose to her throat but she swallowed it back. Had to think like a psychiatrist, not a terrified victim. "Who are you?" she asked, proud that her voice didn't quiver.

"You're so smart with all your degrees—haven't you figured it out, Jenny?"

She frowned at his gruff voice, recognizing the Southern drawl but not quite placing whom the voice belonged to. Not Jamal or Clyde or Carl. Maybe another patient or someone she met recently?

"It's dark in here, I can't see your face," she said, tempering her anger.

A low chuckle rumbled from him, but his tone hardened when he spoke. "After all those long conversations, our private conversations, you should know my voice."

Long conversations? He had been a patient.

"Come on, Jenny, think, darlin'." He squatted down in front of her and twisted a strand of hair between her fingers.

She smelled his strong cologne, a scent that triggered a repulsive memory.

"I remember you, everything about you," he said in a husky voice. "The way you smiled at me the first time I walked into your office. The way your eyes flickered with understanding and kindness." He trailed a finger along her forehead then around her eyes. "You have such kind eyes. Not judgmental. Not harsh or selfish. I knew then that I'd found the one woman in the world who wouldn't abandon me."

Jenny forced her voice to be level. "Because the other women in your life did."

"Yes, but I thought you were different. You promised to be there, to listen, to help me." His voice rattled. "But then you left me just like they had."

Felix Brainard. She knew him now, remembered his outburst at their last session when she'd informed him she was moving. Had her dismissal of him triggered him to kill all those women?

"I didn't abandon you," Jenny said, hoping to stall him although guilt suffused her. Four women had died because of her. "I simply transferred you to Dr. Ragan." Because she'd sensed he was developing an unhealthy attraction/obsession to her. But she'd never imagined he'd follow her.

"That man," Brainard spat out. "He was worthless. And you left me and ran off here to Savannah, then took other men into your care."

"Is that why you came here, Felix?" Jenny asked quietly. "You wanted to see me, to talk to me?"

"Yes," he said, then stroked her face.

A sick chill engulfed Jenny, but she battled a reaction. She wouldn't give him the satisfaction of showing her fear—it would only feed his need for power.

"If you want to talk, why don't you untie me and let's go someplace more comfortable?"

"I like that idea," he said, "the part about going someplace comfortable." He traced a finger along her cheek, the rough pad of his thumb scraping her skin. "In fact we're going to get real comfortable together, Jenny. Before we say goodbye again, we'll know every inch of each other." He licked her jaw. "I've been looking forward to it."

Chapter Seventeen

Raul had phoned the CSI team at Jenny's and asked them to hold Martin if he showed up, then raced to her house. He spotted Martin's white utility van as soon as he turned the curve to Jenny's. He careened into the driveway, parked behind the crime scene van, jumped out and ran up to meet the tech who stood beside the van.

"You were right, Detective Cortez. There were cameras in the house, the living room, bedroom and even the shower."

Raul clenched his jaw and cursed. He was going to kill this bastard when he got hold of him. "Confiscate those cameras, and make sure no one views them. I'll do that personally."

Jordan nodded and went back inside, and Raul strode over to the van. "Mr. Martin, I need you to come with me to the police station."

Martin's bushy eyebrows peeled together. "Why? What's going on?"

"Just come with me, sir. I need to ask you some questions." He took him by the arm and led the man to his car.

"What's this about?" Martin asked, paling.

"I'll explain at the station."

Martin grumbled but climbed in, clasping his hands

together and remaining silent during the ride. When they arrived at the station, Raul escorted him into one of the interrogation rooms, retrieved files of all the Strangler victims.

Sweat beaded on Martin's face and he'd run his hands through his hair, making the gray tufts stand up in a dozen haphazard directions. "This is about Dr. Madden, ain't it?"

Raul nodded. "Yes. Do you know where she is, Martin?"

The man shook his head. "No. When I got to her house that other man told me she was missing, that her house was a crime scene." His gray eyes flickered with worry. "What's happened to her?"

"I thought you might be able to tell us," Raul growled.

Martin winced. "How should I know?"

Raul tossed a photo of each victim on the table, and Martin visibly blanched. "Did you know any of these girls?"

Martin's Adam's apple bobbed as he worked his throat to swallow. "My God…"

"You did know them?"

He nodded, his color paling. "I…did some work at their places."

"And you installed cameras in their houses so you could stalk them?"

His jaw went slack. "No…goodness no, I would never do such a thing."

"You had access to their houses," Raul said bluntly.

Martin dropped his head forward with a groan. "Yes, but I never installed any cameras."

"But your son did?"

"My son?" Martin's voice warbled. "If he did, I didn't know about it."

"He was stalking these women," Raul barked.

"No…" he said in a pained tone. "I mean I didn't realize

it. Hell, I didn't even know I had a son until a few months ago. When he contacted me, he was hard up for money, for a job, so I figured I owed him and let him help me with the renovations."

"So you gave him access to these women's homes?"

Martin pulled at his chin. "I swear I didn't know he'd installed cameras," he screeched. "He was good at repairs, the air-conditioning…"

"And when these girls were murdered, you didn't make the connection?"

"No…" His voice faltered. "I…never thought anything about it. He always left before the women arrived home so they didn't see him."

"You didn't know your son was dangerous?"

Shock strained the man's craggy features, but he hesitated. "I thought he had problems, but I…I didn't think he'd kill anyone."

Raul pounded his fist on the table. "Cut the bull. Jenny Madden's life is in danger. Your son was a patient of hers in Atlanta, and I believe he's here in Savannah, that he's responsible for four women's deaths and that he has Dr. Madden now." He gripped the man by the collar of his work shirt. "He's going to kill her, Martin, unless you tell us where to find him."

Martin bolted up. "Jesus…I don't know where he'd go. He didn't stay with me, only stopped by on the job."

"Do you have a phone number to reach him?"

Martin nodded, and Raul pushed a pad of paper in front of him for Martin to write it down. Raul tried the number, but there was no answer so he rushed out and asked Black to get the tech team to trace it.

Then he stepped back inside the room, his pulse

pounding. "Did your son ever mention another family member or friend? Someone from his past?"

Martin shook his head wildly. "He said he hated his mother for giving him up, that I should have come for him."

That was Brainard's motive. The reason he hated women.

"Who raised him?" Raul asked.

"He grew up in an orphanage," Martin said in a low voice.

"An orphanage here in Savannah?"

He nodded. "Yes. But it's closed now."

The blood roared in Raul's ears. He knew where the orphanage was located. It had been shut down years ago, but the building still stood. Abandoned. Isolated. Off the road and surrounded by woods.

A perfect place to hide. A perfect place to take a victim, because if she screamed, no one would hear her.

"You think of anything else or if he calls in, let me know."

Raul left him in custody, then rushed from the room. Obviously, Brainard blamed Jenny for leaving him as his mother had.

He had to hurry. He couldn't let Brainard kill Jenny....

IT TOOK EVERY OUNCE of Jenny's restraint not to scream as Felix dragged her up the basement steps. A sliver of light wormed its way through the window as he shoved her from the steps down a long corridor which smelled musty and abandoned.

"Where are we?" she asked, stifling a sob as he tightened his hold on her arm.

"I thought you'd want to see where I grew up," he said in a voice laden with anger. "Where my mother left me like I was a shoe she could just throw away."

"I know how much that hurt you," Jenny said.

"You know nothing," Felix chided. "You say you do, but nobody understands what they did to me here. How horrible it was."

"I'd like to hear more, Felix. Now that you're in Savannah, we could set up some regular sessions, start therapy again, one-on-one."

A howl of sinister laughter echoed from his throat. "We're going to have some one-on-one, that's for sure."

Jenny cringed inwardly. "You want someone to understand you, and I'm trying to do that. But I can't understand unless you talk to me. Tell me more about your mother."

"She was cruel and heartless, treated me like crap." He shoved her along. Cobwebs hung tangled along the corridors, a spider spinning its web on the frosted grimy glass, and paint and plaster was waterpocked and peeling from the walls. Somewhere in the distance, a mouse skittered along the floor, birds screeched from the attic and old pipes clanged and groaned.

Jenny struggled for calm. "Did you have friends here, Felix?"

"Friends?" he said in a grating voice. "Not hardly. I learned to be tough, take up for myself 'cause nobody else cared. We were packed in like sardines, everyone scrapping for food. Junk they gave us tasted like mushy cardboard."

They bypassed a large common area that held rotting dilapidated furniture, then he shoved her up a flight of steps and into a dormlike room with rows of metal beds.

"See where we slept at night, all lined up like nobodies?"

Gray walls held more cobwebs and dirty handprints from years gone by.

He pushed her down on one of the beds in the far corner.

"Even with the other boys, every night when I lay in here, I felt so alone. So lonely I wanted to die." His rough fingers raced over her face. "I don't want to be alone anymore." He rubbed his thumb along her cheek again, sending another shudder through her.

"When I met you, I thought I'd found the one person who wouldn't leave me." He rubbed his face along hers. "All those other girls were just a prelude to you, Jenny. You're the one I really wanted. And now we're finally going to be together."

RAUL SWITCHED OFF the lights to his car as he coasted down the wooded drive to the abandoned orphanage. Keegan was supposed to meet him here for backup, but he couldn't wait. He spotted the rear end of a beat-up black sedan poking out from behind the back of the building, a concrete structure overtaken by weeds and overgrown bushes. He crept up the steps and checked the front door. Locked.

Cursing, he circled around and jiggled a basement window open. Wielding his gun, he crawled inside, tearing away cobwebs as he dropped to the floor and inched his way through the basement. It was enough. When he made it to the stairs, he eased up them. The area was dark, yet the door open enough so that a faint beam of light spilled through a small window above the two-story foyer, so high above the floor it was unreachable. He paused to listen, wondering where in the hell Brainard had Jenny, then heard a sinister chuckle echoing off the concrete walls on the second floor.

Inhaling sharply against the pungent odor of decay, dust and mildew, he ascended the winding concrete stairs, the threadbare carpet helping to break the sound.

Then Jenny's voice. "You don't want to do this, Felix.

Let's just slow down and talk. Remember you signed a contract not to hurt anyone."

Good girl, Jenny, keep him talking, Raul mouthed silently. Bracing his gun between both hands, he eased around the corner and down the hall. With no electricity and the mausoleum type structure shadowed by hulking old trees, the place was morbidly dark.

"You promised to take care of me, Jenny, but you broke your promise," Brainard snarled.

"I didn't mean to hurt you, but my mother was sick," Jenny said softly. "There must have been someone in your life who cared for you. A grandmother? A social worker?"

"They said they did, that they cared, then they deserted me, just like you did."

"But I didn't leave you, Felix. And I'm here now and so are you. Let's start over,"

"It's too late for talking." His voice deepened to a growl. "It's time for us to get closer, Jenny. I promise I'll make it good for you. I brought you a cocktail and a new pair of satin panties. I know how you like nice underwear."

Raul ground his teeth. The damn bastard wasn't going to touch her. Barely controlling a roar of rage, he lunged into the room. Through the shadows he spotted Jenny lying on a cot, arms tied above her head to the bedposts. The son of a bitch was beginning to tear at her blouse. "Get away from her now, Brainard, or I'll shoot."

The beefy man swung around with a fierce growl. "No, you leave or I'll kill her."

"I have a gun." Raul stepped forward, his eyes scanning for a weapon. But it was too damn dark to see.

"Raul…" Jenny whispered. "Don't shoot, he has a—"

The blast of a bullet drowned her words. Raul's body

bounced backward, pain ricocheting through his stomach, and his legs spasmed, collapsing beneath him as blood gushed from his abdomen.

"Raul!"

Jenny's cry made his heart clench with a different kind of pain. The muscles in his body protested movement as he fell onto his knees, the room swirling. But he couldn't lose consciousness. Had to save Jenny.

If he died or passed out, Brainard would finish what he'd started.

Raul had lost one woman he loved—he wouldn't lose another.

The room swirled again, darkness begging him to enter its welcoming abyss. Free him of the pain. He had to think. Play it smart. Find a way to win against this bastard.

He called Jenny's name on a groan, then fell forward onto his hands and bowed his head, sucking in oxygen to stem the dizziness.

Thinking he'd won, Brainard reached for Jenny. She screamed as his hands pawed her, and a silver line glinted in the darkness. A needle, the Rohypnol.

Rage rose to his chest, overpowering the pain. Raul lurched forward and ran toward the man. At the same time, Jenny brought her feet up and kicked Brainard in the chest, throwing him backward.

Raul tore him away from Jenny, then threw him to the floor, pounding him in the face and abdomen. Brainard fought back, and the two of them tumbled and rolled. Raul's side split with pain, but he crawled forward, latched his fingers onto his gun, then brought it back and slammed it into Brainard's head. Brainard grunted, then fell backward, his head hitting the metal poles of the bed.

Raul hit him again and again, digging the barrel of the gun into his throat.

"Raul, please stop," Jenny whispered. "Please don't kill him."

Somewhere in the back of his mind, her words registered, pain and fear ripping at his conscience. If he killed Brainard, he wouldn't get to send him to prison.

Death was too easy and quick for the sadistic sicko.

Grinding his teeth against the pain, he checked for a pulse. Brainard was alive but out cold.

"Raul…please…"

He dragged himself away, the room spinning as he crawled toward her. Blindly he untied her hands and feet, running his hands over her face. "Jenny, God, are you okay?"

"I am now," she whispered. "But you've been hit."

"I love you," he said on a choked breath. Then he fell into her arms and the darkness consumed him.

"RAUL!" JENNY SCREAMED and tried to lift him, but blood pooled onto the mattress and he was unconscious. She had to get help.

Suddenly footsteps thundered from below, and Detective Keegan ran in. "Help me," Jenny cried. "Raul's been shot."

He took one look at Brainard on the floor, then Raul and hurried to Brainard and secured him as he called for an ambulance.

Tears streamed down her face, and fear for Raul engulfed her. Raul had whispered that he loved her before he passed out, but she hadn't said the words in return.

She did love him, but it was her fault he'd been shot. Her fault all those women had died. Her fault…

The detective rushed to her, turned Raul onto his back

and saw the blood. Quickly he tore a faded pillowcase off the bed, then pressed it to Raul's wound.

Outside a siren pierced the air, shrill and coming closer.

"Are you hurt?" Detective Keegan asked.

"No." She rubbed at her raw wrists dotted with blood themselves, but waved off his concern as she pulled Raul's head into her lap. He was so pale and ashen looking, and there was so much blood. She loved him so much....

She couldn't lose him.

Chapter Eighteen

The next few hours were the longest of Jenny's life. She rode in the ambulance with Raul, clutching his hand as they transported him to the hospital. As soon as they arrived, the staff whisked him into surgery, then treated the abrasions on her wrists and ankles.

Detective Keegan and Captain Black approached her as she sat in the waiting room huddled in a blanket.

Keegan handed her a cup of coffee which she cradled in her hands, sipping slowly and hoping her stomach could tolerate the caffeine.

"Did you hear yet?" she asked.

Keegan shook his head. "He'll make it, Dr. Madden. Raul's one of the toughest men I know."

She nodded, praying he was right. Captain Black sat down beside her, his expression grave. "We have everything we need to nail Brainard for a long time. Blood on the floor in Machete's house was Judy Benson's, and Brainard's prints were all over the house. A splinter under her finger was traced to the paint Martin used. And the tapes of the crimes show him in action. We also found tapes of the girls in their homes, and the stash of underwear he bought to use on the victims along with the trophy pieces he took."

Jenny gasped, then met his gaze and saw the truth in his eyes. "You found hidden cameras in my house?"

He nodded. "I'm sorry. But it appears Brainard was the long-lost son of Ralph Martin. Martin let him come during the day and help with the painting. That gave him access to your house."

"Ralph had worked for the other girls?"

Again, he nodded. "There's more, Jenny. I don't know if Raul had a chance to tell you but we have your brother in custody."

"What?" Her heart sank, worry piling upon guilt and fear for Raul.

He explained that Bailey had visited her mother and caught Dr. Zovall in the act of trying to drug her and had pulled a knife. "We arrested Zovall. He admitted that he broke into your place and tried to strangle you because he was afraid you'd find out what he'd done to your mother and expose him."

Jenny's breath caught. "Is Mom all right?"

"Your mother is fine. Bailey saved her."

"Are you pressing charges against Bailey?"

Black folded his hands. "No, but he was pretty upset."

"He needs a drug treatment program," Jenny agreed. "And some serious counseling."

"I'm sure you'll see that he gets it."

Yes, she would do everything she could for her mother and brother, but the next few months wouldn't be easy.

The surgeon appeared in the doorway. "We're finished with Detective Cortez. He's in recovery now."

"How is he?" Captain Black asked.

"He'll be sore and need some rest, but he'll make it."

Jenny finally released the breath she'd been holding. "Can we see him?"

"For just a moment."

Jenny glanced at Keegan and the captain, but they motioned for her to go in. Her stomach fluttered as she entered the recovery area, tears threatening at the sight of the bandage on Raul's abdomen and the sickly pallor of his skin.

His eyes flickered open, and he tried to move his hand as if to reach for her. She went to him, grasped it between her own and the tears fell.

"I'm so sorry, Raul, I was so worried about you," she cried. "It was all my fault, Felix Brainard killed those women because of me. And he almost killed you, too."

He squeezed her hand and shook his head. "Don't, Jenny. Not your fault."

But it was her fault, she thought silently. Raul had blamed the other doctor for his wife's death, and now he'd almost lost his life because of her. Because of the job she'd insisted was her way of helping people. But she'd helped no one, only brought pain and death into her life as well as to four innocent girls.

She didn't know how she could ever forgive herself.

NIGHT HAD FALLEN when Raul finally awakened, and he wondered at the time. How long had he been here? Hours? Days?

He checked his watch and realized it had been two days. Two days since Jenny had been by his side.

It felt like forever. He remembered her taking his hand in the recovery room, the agony and guilt in her voice. By now she must know he'd arrested Bailey and Dr. Zovall, and he wanted to explain his reasoning.

He had to see her. Tell her the truth. Assure her he loved her and convince her that none of this was her fault.

Jenny had the sweetest soul of anyone on earth, and he needed her.

He shoved off the covers, wincing at the pain in his abdomen, then yanked the IV from his arm. Suddenly the door opened, and Bailey Madden walked in, his hands shoved in the pockets of his faded baggy jeans.

Raul braced himself for whatever the boy had to say. "What are you doing here, Bailey?"

"I came to talk to you, to apologize," he said in a low voice.

Raul leaned back against the pillows. "I figured you were still pissed."

"I was," he admitted. "But I had time to calm down in that cell."

"That was the point," Raul said. "I don't blame you for attacking that doctor. He deserved it."

Bailey's gaze shot to his.

"I'm not condoning your behavior, kid. I think you've had a lot dumped on you and you need help."

Bailey's expression turned contrite. "That's why I came. I just saw Jenny and told her I'm checking myself into a treatment program. I'm going to try my damnedest to clean up my act and make something of myself. Someone she can be proud of."

"That's good," Raul said. "You can be anything you want, you just have to work at it."

Bailey didn't look quite convinced, but at least he was on the right path.

"I heard you saved my sister's life."

Raul shrugged. "I was doing my job."

Bailey arched a brow. The kid had gotten a haircut and shaved, almost looked decent.

"It's more than that," Bailey said. "There's something going on between you two, isn't there?"

He refused to lie. "I'm in love with your sister, Bailey. I don't know how she feels, but I want to keep seeing her."

"Have you told Jenny?"

He shook his head. "No, she hasn't been back." He swung his legs over the side of the bed. "I need to see her though, tonight."

Bailey grinned. "You need a ride?"

Raul nodded. "Just let me find some damn clothes."

His stitches pulled as he threw off the hospital gown and tugged on the T-shirt.

Raul fumbled with the jeans but managed to pull them on. Forgoing socks, he shoved his feet into his shoes and shuffled toward the door.

He staggered slightly, and Bailey helped him sneak past the personnel, down the hall, to the elevator and to his car. The bumpy ride further agitated the ache in his gut, and he clutched his abdomen, hoping he didn't rip the stitches. He didn't want to show up bloody on Jenny's doorstep.

A few minutes later Bailey pulled up in front of Jenny's. Night was falling, and lights burned brightly throughout Jenny's house. Black had visited Raul in the hospital and told him that he'd informed Jenny about the cameras. Every time he thought about the man violating her, he wished he'd killed Brainard and left him in a puddle of his own filthy blood.

"Well, I'd better get going," Bailey said. "I gotta check in tonight."

"Good luck, Bailey." Raul extended his hand and Jenny's brother shook it. "If I can help you in any way, just call."

Emotions clouded the young man's eyes, and he thanked him, then drove away.

Holding his hand to his bandaged wound, Raul forced his feet to move up the drive, then the steps to the porch. Hoping she didn't turn him away, he punched the bell.

One ring. Two. Three. Finally he heard footsteps. He saw her check the peephole, and noted the sign for the alarm system on the door. Thank God. He should have insisted she install one from the beginning. Hell, he should have installed one for her.

The door squeaked open and he sucked in a deep breath.

"Raul?" Her voice was a bare whisper in the balmy air. "Is it really you?"

"Yes, honey, it's me. In the flesh."

Tears spilled over, and she chewed her bottom lip. "What are you doing out of the hospital? You shouldn't be up."

"I had to see you," he said gruffly when all he wanted to do was pull her into his arms. "Can I come in?"

Uncertainty and pain registered on her pretty face, but she gestured for him to enter. He followed her to the den, and she ordered him to sit down, but he insisted she sit, too.

"I can't believe you came, after all I put you through," she said in a tortured whisper.

"Jenny, stop." He clutched her hands between his own. "When you didn't come back, I thought you might be upset with me. That you didn't want to see me anymore."

"I couldn't face you," she said, pain in her eyes. "You were right about me, about my job. Those women died because of me."

"No," he said emphatically. "They died because of a sick man, Jenny."

"One *I* was supposed to help."

"Ahh, honey, you tried. But a very smart lady once told me that we save some but we can't save them all. We're all human, so cut yourself some slack."

Her body trembled, then her gaze met his.

"I wanted to explain about Bailey," he said gruffly. "The reason I locked him up that night."

"You thought he was the Strangler?"

He shook his head. "No…well, we found links to MySpace accounts that were traced to the other victims. We assumed Bailey had that account, since it was tied to your computer. Now we know that Brainard set up the account when he gained access to your house through his father."

Her cheeks colored with bitterness. "When he installed cameras in my house to watch me."

He gulped back his own mixture of anger and disgust. "Yes."

She nodded, then angled her head away with a shudder. "How many people have viewed those tapes, Raul?"

"No one," he said emphatically. "I gave the CSI team strict orders when I discovered them that I was the only one to see them."

She lifted her head, a mixture of emotions in her eyes. "I don't want them to get out."

"I promise you that they won't. We don't have to show them in order to convict Brainard. I'll destroy them myself."

Her chin quivered. "Thank you, Raul."

She started to stand as if to dismiss him. To send him away. He couldn't allow that. "Don't thank me," he said gruffly. "I don't want anyone else seeing my wife naked but me."

Her luminous eyes flickered in surprise. "What?"

"I love you, Jenny." His voice cracked as he pulled her back down beside him. "Do you have any idea how terrified I was when you were missing? I thought I'd die from fear. Kept imagining what he might be doing to you, and I wanted to rip his throat apart with my bare hands." His blood pressure was spiking. "I can't lose you, honey." He lifted her hands and kissed them. "I won't. I need you."

"But so much happened. I'm a mess, Raul. So is my family." She gestured around the house. "I'm not even sure I want to stay here. I was so excited about renovating this place, but knowing the man who helped fix it up was the father of the Strangler, knowing that he watched me here... I'm not sure it'll ever feel like home."

"We'll do whatever you want about the house. Live here, buy another one, it doesn't matter to me where we are, as long as we're together."

"Raul..."

"Shh. I'm not rushing you. Take all the time you need, Jenny. We can figure things out together." His voice thickened with emotions. "Just let me be with you. Don't shut me out." He tilted her chin up with his thumb. "I want to be in your life. Forever."

A small flicker of a smile teased her beautiful eyes. "I don't know what I'm going to do about my job, either," she said softly.

His jaw tightened. He'd have to support any decision she made if she was going to be his wife. But, God, the thought of another sicko fixating on her terrified him.

"I don't think I can keep doing what I've been doing," she admitted on a sigh.

He cupped her face in his hands. "Jenny, don't leave

your job because you think you failed Brainard. You're a wonderful doctor and you've helped a lot of people."

She nodded slowly. "Maybe, but I want to take some time off for my mom and brother, and for myself. And I'm thinking that when I return, I may try working with young people. Maybe I can reach them before they get so screwed up." She hesitated, then cleared her throat, determination in her voice when she spoke again. "I don't want to live the rest of my life with my family in danger because of my patients."

His breath whooshed out. He hoped that family included him. "I can't say as I'm not relieved. I thought I might have to turn in my badge and become your permanent bodyguard."

A glint sparkled in her eyes. "You could still be my permanent bodyguard."

He grinned and leaned toward her, cradling her face between his hands. "Does that mean you'll marry me? Be my wife?"

She pressed a kiss to his lips, the sweetest moment he'd ever known. "Yes. Your wife, your lover, your friend." Then she pulled away and looked into his face, tears glittering on her lashes. "And the mother of your children, if you want."

His heart burst with happiness and a deep love for this woman. He would always love his first wife, but she would want him to go on, to love again.

He wiggled his eyebrows, took her hands in his. "Maybe we should start practicing now."

She laughed, a whimsical sound that was so beautiful it sounded like wind chimes. "But you're injured, Raul."

"I know and I need some TLC." He pulled her to her feet

and led her toward the stairs. "You'll just have to be gentle with me tonight, not that animal that you usually are."

She laughed again, and he knew they were going to be all right, that he had found his soul mate and the love of his life.

Epilogue

Six Months Later

The wedding vows had been exchanged along with the rings, and the reception was winding down.

Jenny's mother wrapped her into a warm hug. "I love you so much, sweetheart. I'm so proud that you've found a wonderful man to love."

"And I'm so proud to have you here with me, Mom." Tears threatened again, but she blinked them back. She and her mother and Bailey had shared a lot of heartfelt emotions and tears over the past few months. But both her mother and Bailey had made tremendous progress. Bailey had committed to his drug treatment program and, because of Raul's influence, had enrolled in school again. He'd even talked about becoming a policeman like Raul one day.

Guitar music drifted through the reception room, and she smiled, grateful Raul's family had made it to the wedding. Raul loped up, grinning from ear to ear. He'd been catching up with his boisterous loving family who had welcomed her with open arms.

"Are you about ready to leave, Mrs. Cortez?"

She nodded, tucked her arm in his, and they ran through the crowd to a limo Raul had rented to drive them to their honeymoon suite. The next day they'd fly to Hawaii for a week where they planned to do nothing but relax on the beach all day and make love all night.

As soon as they got in the hotel suite, they tore off each other's clothes and made frenzied love. She sighed and rolled over into his arms. She'd never get tired of loving him, of looking at him.

"Happy?" he asked.

She grinned and traced a finger over his chest. "Yes. I have my family back, and you've made me happier than I ever thought I could be."

"I love you, Jenny. I always will."

"I love you, too."

He kissed her thoroughly and Jenny held him close, still afraid she'd lose him, that her life was too good to be true.

"We forgot about the champagne," he murmured against her ear. "Want a toast now?"

He started to reach for the bottle on the nightstand but she caught his arm. "I'd better not, Raul. It's not good for the baby."

His dark eyes widened, and moisture glistened in his eyes. "Baby?"

She laid her hand against his cheek. "It's not too soon, is it?"

He cleared his throat, worked his mouth side to side as if struggling for words, yet his eyes reflected emotions. "Before…I thought I didn't deserve to be a father…"

Her heart clenched, and she placed his hand on her belly. "You do, Raul. And I want to give you a baby, for us to have a big family of our own."

He kissed her again, this time so tenderly that tears filled her eyes. When he pulled away, he laid his head down on her belly, and she stroked his hair.

"I promise to be a good father," he whispered to the child growing inside her. "And to always be around for you and your mother."

Jenny closed her eyes and thanked the heavens for this man. She'd finally found a man who loved her completely, one who would never leave her, and she intended to savor every moment.

* * * * *

Look for more BENEATH THE BADGE *by reader favorite Rita Herron in August 2008, only from Harlequin Intrigue!*

THOROUGHBRED LEGACY
The stakes are high when it comes to love,
horse racing, family secrets
and broken promises.

A new exciting Harlequin continuity series coming soon!
Led by New York Times *bestselling author*
Elizabeth Bevarly
FLIRTING WITH TROUBLE

Here's a preview!

THE DOOR CLOSED behind them, throwing them into darkness and leaving them utterly alone. And the next thing Daniel knew, he heard himself saying, "Marnie, I'm sorry about the way things turned out in Del Mar."

She said nothing at first, only strode across the room and stared out the window beside him. Although he couldn't see her well in the darkness—he still hadn't switched on a light…but then, neither had she—he imagined her expression was a little preoccupied, a little anxious, a little confused.

Finally, very softly, she said, "Are you?"

He nodded, then, worried she wouldn't be able to see the gesture, added, "Yeah. I am. I should have said goodbye to you."

"Yes, you should have."

Actually, he thought, there were a lot of things he should have done in Del Mar. He'd had *a lot* riding on the Pacific Classic, and even more on his entry, Little Joe, but after meeting Marnie, the Pacific Classic had been the last thing on Daniel's mind. His loss at Del Mar had pretty much ended his career before it had even begun, and he'd had to start all over again, rebuilding from nothing.

He simply had not then and did not now have room in his life for a woman as potent as Marnie Roberts. He was a horseman first and foremost. From the time he was a schoolboy, he'd known what he wanted to do with his life—be the best possible trainer he could be.

He had to make sure Marnie understood—and he understood, too—why things had ended the way they had eight years ago. He just wished he could find the words to do that. Hell, he wished he could find the *thoughts* to do that.

"You made me forget things, Marnie, things that I really needed to remember. And that scared the hell out of me. Little Joe should have won the Classic. He was by far the best horse entered in that race. But I didn't give him the attention he needed and deserved that week, because all I could think about was you. Hell, when I woke up that morning all I wanted to do was lie there and look at you, and then wake you up and make love to you again. If I hadn't left when I did—the way I did—I might still be lying there in that bed with you, thinking about nothing else."

"And would that be so terrible?" she asked.

"Of course not," he told her. "But that wasn't why I was in Del Mar," he repeated. "I was in Del Mar to win a race. That was my job. And my work was the most important thing to me."

She said nothing for a moment, only studied his face in the darkness as if looking for the answer to a very important question. Finally she asked, "And what's the most important thing to you now, Daniel?"

Wasn't the answer to that obvious? "My work," he answered automatically.

She nodded slowly. "Of course," she said softly. "That is, after all, what you do best."

Her comment, too, puzzled him. She made it sound as if being good at what he did was a bad thing.

She bit her lip thoughtfully, her eyes fixed on his, glimmering in the scant moonlight that was filtering through the window. And damned if Daniel didn't find himself wanting to pull her into his arms and kiss her. But as much as it might have felt as if no time had passed since Del Mar, there were eight years between now and then. And eight years was a long time in the best of circumstances. For Daniel and Marnie, it was virtually a lifetime.

So Daniel turned and started for the door, then halted. He couldn't just walk away and leave things as they were, unsettled. He'd done that eight years ago and regretted it.

"It *was* good to see you again, Marnie," he said softly. And since he was being honest, he added, "I hope we see each other again."

She didn't say anything in response, only stood silhouetted against the window with her arms wrapped around her in a way that made him wonder whether she was doing it because she was cold, or if she just needed something—someone—to hold on to. In either case, Daniel understood. There was an emptiness clinging to him that he suspected would be there for a long time.

* * * * *

THOROUGHBRED LEGACY
coming soon wherever books are sold!

Thoroughbred Legacy

Launching in June 2008

A dramatic new 12-book continuity that embodies the American Dream.

Meet the Prestons, owners of Quest Stables, a successful horse-racing and breeding empire. But the lives, loves and reputations of this hardworking family are put at risk when a breeding scandal unfolds.

Flirting with Trouble

by *New York Times* bestselling author

ELIZABETH BEVARLY

Eight years ago, publicist Marnie Roberts spent seven days of bliss with Australian horse trainer Daniel Whittleson. But just as quickly, he disappeared. Now Marnie is heading to Australia to finally confront the man she's never been able to forget.

The stakes are high when it comes to love, horse racing, family secrets and broken promises.

A new exciting Harlequin continuity series coming soon!

Royal Seductions

Michelle Celmer delivers a powerful miniseries in
Royal Seductions; where two brothers fight for the
crown and discover love. In *The King's Convenient Bride*,
the king discovers his marriage of convenience to the
woman he's been promised to wed is turning all too
real. The playboy prince proposes a mock engagement
to defuse rumors circulating about him and restore
order to the kingdom…until his pretend fiancée
becomes pregnant in *The Illegitimate Prince's Baby*.

Look for

THE KING'S CONVENIENT BRIDE
&
THE ILLEGITIMATE PRINCE'S BABY

BY MICHELLE CELMER

Available in June 2008 wherever you buy books.

Always Powerful, Passionate and Provocative.

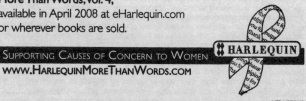

REQUEST YOUR FREE BOOKS!

2 FREE NOVELS PLUS 2 FREE GIFTS!

HARLEQUIN®

INTRIGUE®

Breathtaking Romantic Suspense

HI08

NEW YORK TIMES
BESTSELLING AUTHOR

ANNE
STUART

Talk about lost in translation....

In the wake of a failed love affair, Jilly Lovitz takes off for
Tokyo. She's expecting to cry on her sister Summer's shoulder,
then spend a couple months blowing off steam in Japan.
Instead, she's snatched away on the back of a motorcycle,
narrowly avoiding a grisly execution attempt meant for her
sister and brother-in-law.

Her rescuer is Reno. They'd met before and the attraction was
odd but electric. Now Reno and Jilly are pawns in a deadly
tangle of assassination attempts, kidnappings and prisoner
swaps that could put their steamy partnership on ice.

FIRE AND ICE

"Anne Stuart delivers exciting stuff for those of us who like
our romantic suspense dark and dangerous."
—*New York Times* bestselling author Jayne Ann Krentz

*Available the first week of May 2008
wherever paperbacks are sold!*

MIRA®

www.MIRABooks.com

MAS2536

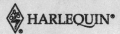

INTRIGUE®

COMING NEXT MONTH

www.eHarlequin.com

HICNM0508R